Embracing the Light

By Inez Brinkley

©2006 by Inez Brinkley

First Printing

ISBN: 978-1-4116-9827-7

Published by Lulu Publishing

www.lulu.com

Printed in the United States of America

REVIEW

It is a privilege to review this story. I haven't read a page turner like this in years! The story kept me riveted to my seat wondering just how Joseph and Jennie were to find Joshua. Of course I never doubted the IF, but that is a matter of faith. The surprise, is the "who, how, and where?" The characters and plot are well developed, and the story line flows easily, even with flashbacks.

We are all tested at some time, and "Embracing the Light" shows how even the strongest of us can be tested, but we know that He will never forsake us.

I give "Embracing the Light" FIVE crosses (better than stars) and look forward to reading the rest of Inez' work. If you want an interesting read, then Inez Brinkley's "Embracing the Light" will keep you riveted.

(Warning! If you want a bedtime story to put you to sleep, try something else. This is just too good to put down. Although on a weekend, you will sleep well afterwards.)

David Cristwell
Author of "Auroraview, Alaska"

DEDICATION

This book is dedicated to all of my loyal friends and relatives who stood behind me through my first book, and who stand with me now. And it's also dedicated to my husband Gerald who supports me in all that I do. Last but always first; it is dedicated to my Lord Jesus. Without Him, there would not have been any books written.

Web Site: www.embracingthelight.homestead.com

As I was writing this book, God spoke to me in chapter fourteen. He said that Joseph, the main character in the book, is a parallel of Himself. No matter where Jennie goes, no matter what she does to Joseph, yet he loves her with an all-consuming love. Nothing can destroy it or change it. What she does and what she says will not affect his love.

And that is how the Lord's love is for us. It doesn't matter where we go, what we do, what we say or think, He loves us with an ALL CONSUMING LOVE.

And nothing on earth or in Heaven can change that.

And the gates of hell will not prevail against it.

A Word About Demons....

Although demons are very real, and very prevalent in this world we live in, I have taken a few liberties with facts about demons in my book. I don't believe that a real demon can physically pick us up as described in this book. Since I have seen demons and angels at times in my Christian walk, I think a lot of the information is accurate. Of course the descriptions of the ones with faces is strictly fictional, as well as the ones with bird like wings. Just keep in mind that this is a fiction novel but God can use it to teach us things we didn't know about demons and angels if we will just keep our hearts and minds saturated in Jesus Christ.

"I Will Sing To My Beloved"

"You sing songs of praise to Me, My child, and I want to sing songs of love to you. For you are My creation and My joy. I will speak countless words to you if you will hear. I will sing to My beloved, words of love from My heart.

Listen – I speak, I sing. I am here. Seek Me for the words I speak bring life and joy.

My written word speaks volumes. Seek Me daily in it. Yet learn to listen for My songs of love to you.

I am ever by your side. Why do you feel lonely and afraid? For I am here love. Just hold My hand and let Me walk with you every day. Don't let the ups and downs of life rule you. Seek Me and walk in My joy for I am the joy giver.

I bring refreshing to your soul. I long, long, long to fellowship with you daily. My heart breaks when you ignore Me.

Come child, hold My hand. Feel My love. Enter My joy.

Come, let us dance in the sunlight. Let My love flow freely into your heart.

Let your path become My path. Let us walk it together. Come, My love."

Chapter One

The moonlight bathed her body in a soft white light, and Jennie seemed to glow with an inner glow. She walked quickly, as fast as her large cumbersome body would allow. She put her hands on her stomach as a small sharp pain hit her.

"Oh no Joshua, you can't come yet. I have two months to go." She spoke lovingly to the baby within her.

She was going as fast as she could because she knew Joseph would be worried about her. He didn't like her going out on a mission by herself, especially at night. But the deliverance took longer than she had thought it would.

Normally they scheduled these ministry times when they could both go, but Andrea had sounded desperate. She was suicidal and Jennie didn't want to take any chances. In the past, Jennie had delivered her of a bunch of demons, some there since childhood. People pick up all kinds of spirits through life—the world liked to call them phobias, habits, but Jennie called them what they were: demons.

Now Andrea had a chance at life, a chance to live normally and be happy. Jennie met Andrea through a stripper she knew from Bourbon Street. Jennie knew many of them because that was her main ministry, bringing salvation to them, then deliverance.

She thought about Joseph and her face lit up in a radiant smile. He was the love of her life; in fact, he was her life. They had only been married a year but the passion they felt for each other still exploded with just a kiss. She flushed just thinking about him. He was almost six-foot tall; his thick blonde hair always seemed to fall in the middle of his forehead in a curl. He had the deepest blue eyes that she had ever seen. She could drown in his eyes when they looked at each other. She thought about his muscular arms crushing her to him, and she walked faster. She couldn't wait to be held in his arms.

Theirs was a love that couldn't be blotted out by all the forces of hell. The devil had tried hard to keep them apart, but God had a destiny for them, and it was to serve together. Moreover, God had revealed to them that their son Joshua would be the deliverer of the next generation.

She saw them all around her, high up in the trees, perched like big fat vultures. They knew they couldn't bother her because she was protected by the power of God, and His angels were always around, watching over her. Nevertheless, they watched and waited, hoping that one day she would slip up, forsake God, and they would be right there to enter her.

These demons had patience for they were ancient, eternal, around since the beginning of time. They freely roamed the streets looking for a nice warm body to inhabit. They loved warm bodies and hated to be cast into the dry places, that hot, arid place of hell where they came from.

Jennie walked up her sidewalk to the apartment building they lived in on Dauphine Street. Before she could even open the door, Joseph flung it open and pulled her into his arms, as best he could with that cumbersome bundle between them.

"Oh God, Jennie! I was so worried. You promised me you wouldn't go out alone at night. You know the dangers out there."

"I know, my love, but this was really an emergency. Andrea was suicidal and I was afraid to take a chance on not going there."

"Then you should have called me at the Precinct and I would've taken you there." He said as he caressed her back.

"I hate to bother you at work. You never know what cases you'll be working on and I just don't want to be one of those pesky wives always bugging their husband at work."

"I want you to bug me. I loathe every second we're apart." His lips found hers, and their passion for each other was ignited. "Oh Jennie, what on earth would I do without you?" He patted her huge belly, "And without him."

Joseph watched her as she fixed supper and set the table. Even after a year of marriage, he was still astounded by her beauty. Long thick black hair softly curling below her shoulders, emerald green eyes, and pouty lips that seemed to beg to be kissed. Even heavy with child she was still desirable to him, still the most beautiful woman he had ever met.

He shuddered when he thought about the past, when he almost lost her. She would have been the next victim the cult would have sacrificed to Satan if God hadn't shown Joseph where to find her. It was all a painful memory now. Gary, the one who kidnapped her, was safely in prison—on death row for murder. Even though that was in the past and Gary couldn't possibly get to her now, he still worried about her whenever she was out of his sight. Especially at night—going off on some deliverance mission.

God had called them to battle the demonic spirits that were rapidly taking over the world. They were on the verge of end times and it was becoming obvious in world situations, even if he and Jennie had not seen personally the increased amount of demonic activity.

There was a new president in the White House now, and he was definitely not a conservative as the former president had been. He was not concerned with bringing morals back to the world. He pushed agendas that said everyone could do their own thing, and religion was a crutch that would slowly be taken out of the world.

The world itself was on the verge of a nuclear war but Christians already knew that the world would end by fire. The earth was on a destructive course and times and epochs were quickly scrolling backward. Since the beginning of time, events had unfolded like a scroll, so it was normal for the scroll to turn back to its original direction.

Joseph and Jennie had to bring their Bible Study underground for fear of reprisal from the liberal groups who were harassing Christians. People were already reporting Bible study groups all over the city to these liberals, and many Bible studies were stopped. Theirs secretly met in an old warehouse on South Peters Street, three blocks from the river; a warehouse that their friends Jim and Barbara Buford had graciously provided.

New Orleans—that city of Voodoo and witchcraft was overseen by the major principality—the spirit of python. He was their old nemesis and both she and Joseph had done battle with him in the past. He had squads of other demons under him, and there were squads of common demons under those that roamed the earth, looking for bodies to inhabit. Those who were not sealed by the blood of Christ were already open portals for demons, and when they committed sin, more came in.

The elite few, those bought with the Blood, were organized throughout the city to rescue those who wanted to be set free from the bondage of the demonic. These elite had Guardian Angels watching over them and protecting them so that demons could not harass them.

Many churches had already gone underground because of the state the world was in, and the way politicians were talking about a one-world religion. They were trying to take Jesus Christ out of religion and pushed other gods—unholy gods as their agenda. It was commonplace to hear of satanic cults popping up everywhere. To be sure, human sacrifice was still against the law, but who knew where it would go in the future.

It sure made Joseph's job harder. He was a vice cop and the courts were getting so lenient with crooks, protecting their rights and all, that it was harder to get them prosecuted.

He still worked at the First District Precinct on North Rampart Street under Captain Parmeter. They had worked together during the big bust when they rounded up those involved in the satanic ritual murders. After the smoke cleared and those involved were quick to point a finger; even the Police Commissioner was arrested. He was later charged with accessory to murder.

Jennie let out a soft moan and doubled over.

"Is it time?" Joseph asked nervously.

"No, I think he's just kicking up a storm and anxious to get out of there. He probably wants to get out so he can kick some demon butts."

Joseph laughed. "That's my boy!"

Sleep was a long time coming to Jennie that night. She was miserable no matter how she lay in bed. She didn't want to keep Joseph awake so she went into the living room and lay down on the sofa. Her back was hurting and she was having Braxton Hicks contractions, false labor. She knew it wasn't Joshua's time to be born yet.

She finally drifted off into a deep sleep and, for the first time, she had the "dream", which is how she referred to it from that night on. She was in that same swirling mist she remembered from another dream she'd had over a year ago, but the mist lifted in this one and she saw a lot of different evil faces leering at her. They were surrounding her, forming a circle around her. The faces were not like the demonic faces she had encountered in the past. It was as if someone had painted the faces on people and made them all different for variety. Some were monster faces, some animal, but she felt the evil in them, and knew that they meant her harm. She started screaming as they danced around her and wasn't aware that she was screaming out loud.

Joseph came running, gun in hand, to protect the woman he loved. When he saw that she was in the throes of a nightmare, he took her in his arms and gently shook her. "Jennie, honey, wake up. It's only a dream. I'm here now and this time, I'll always be here for you."

She opened her eyes and looked wildly about, expecting to see a circle of evil faces around her. When she saw that she was safe and Joseph held her in his arms, she clung to him and sobbed, a sound of anguish that broke his heart.

"Oh Joseph, this was worse than the black swirling mist that I dreamed of last time. My life was in danger; the life of Joshua was in danger. The evil, it was so real, so prevalent in the dream. Hold me Joseph."

He tightened his grip on her. "Nothing will ever harm you or our child, I promise you that. Just promise me that you won't go out alone at night any more."

She nodded. "I promise."

The ominous figures watched them—always there—hoping for a chance to enter them and control these two warriors of God. Especially now that they were to have a son—a greater warrior than the two of these. "We'll have to watch these two always," one of the demons said. "There will be a time when they are not protected by God's Holy

Angels. Then we will slip in and bring them down. And their destruction will be great."

However, unknown to them, God's angels were watching also. They could not see God's angels unless the angels themselves chose to be seen, and usually that was only when the angels were going to do battle with them.

"These fallen angels are foolish," one of the angels said. "They should know that we, as their guardian angels, will never leave them alone, to be at the mercy of Lucifer. We will always stand guard over them, no matter where they go or what they do. For they have a destiny in the Lord."

Chapter Two

As Joseph left for work the next day, an uneasiness descended upon him. He didn't want to tell Jennie, but her dream really upset him. He remembered so well the other dream she'd had and it had come true. He knew that the evil that lurked in the corners of their life was always hatching up new ways to kill them or do whatever harm they could. The demonic forces had succeeded in keeping him and Jennie apart and he almost lost her. He couldn't bear it if anything happened to her.

"It's funny," he thought, "my co-workers used to call me the 'ice man' because I didn't show or feel any emotions. Well I'm certainly feeling them now. Jennie has changed my whole life, turned it completely around and upside down!"

Captain Parmeter came into the squad room late that day. "Ok folks, we got a dead one; they found a body on Decatur Street. Let's move it gentlemen. Go do your best investigating."

Joseph put his reports away and put his gun back in its holster. "Looks like another busy night," he thought. "But at least it will take my mind off of worrying about Jennie." He wondered if their world would ever be safe again. Then he realized how stupid that thought was. Just looking around and seeing all the demons hanging out, he knew that life as they knew it would never be safe again.

Decatur Street was already bustling with cops when he arrived. The uniformed cops had placed crime scene tape around the scene. He went over to where the corpse lay face down on the sidewalk and saw that it was a young woman. The scene brought back memories of earlier scenes with other dead women, and for a moment, he was catapulted back in time. He thought about beautiful Elise, her body pulled from the river, skin all pale and washed out like a dead fish. And he thought about Janna, Elise's friend. She was killed because he had talked to her and questioned her about the guy Elise was with on her last night alive.

He didn't like to think about Janna because he felt such guilt. She would probably still be alive if he hadn't questioned her about Gary. "Who do we have here?" He asked the officer who had cordoned off the area.

"No ID's been made yet. I haven't even seen her face. We're waiting for the photographer to get here."

Ray the police photographer walked up at that moment. "What's that, you're waiting for me? You oughta give a person time to make the drive here and get his equipment in order. Ok, flip her over."

They turned the body over and Joseph audibly gasped. It was the girl who finally told him that Elise had been with Gary on that fateful night. He had walked up to her and flung her against the wall, telling her she didn't have to fear the killer, now she had to fear him. She had seen in his eyes that he was desperate and told him what he wanted to know. Now, a year later she was dead.

"But no way could it be related," he thought to himself. "It's been a year. This is just a weird coincidence."

"So you know her, huh?" Ray questioned. "Friend of yours?"

"Yeah, I met her before, but no, she's not exactly a friend. It just threw me for a loop to see her lying here dead. Any sign of how she died?"

"No, we'll let the ME answer that one. You can probably call him tomorrow and he'll have something to tell you."

The forensic people were hard at work, scouring every inch of the crime scene. It took a lot of cooperation between departments to get it all together. Nevertheless, all the reports would be filed and put on computer. Then he could read each one to try to piece together what happened.

Joseph saw increased demonic activity in this area. It was known as a high crime area and many dead bodies were just dropped off here after they were murdered somewhere else. He wondered about the stripper. "Was she killed where she lay, or was she just dumped here?

Please God; don't let it be a ritual murder." There were too many bad memories attached to the past.

It was after dark and he knew Jennie would be worried so he pulled out his cell phone and called her. "Hi sweetheart, listen, I'm gonna be a little late tonight. We got this case we have to work on. No more labor pains huh?"

"Just a few—but they don't mean anything. You be careful my love. Is there a lot of demonic activity there?"

"Yeah, a whole lot. Can you imagine a world without it?" He asked.

"No, but I know that there will be one day. When the Lord destroys this world and creates the new one, it will be totally free of demons. Won't that be nice? Promise me you'll be careful."

"You know I will," he laughed. "I have a lot to live for these days. I'll see you later tonight. If you get tired, don't wait up for me. Joshua needs his rest."

For some reason he didn't want to tell her about the stripper. There was probably no connection whatsoever, but he didn't want to give her anything to worry about.

He didn't want to wait until morning to find out how she died, so he followed the ambulance to the morgue. He knew the ME would still be there working on other cases, trying to catch up. New Orleans was the murder capital of the U.S. and kept Joe and his crew busy all hours.

He followed the EMT's into the morgue with their load and sure enough, Joe was still working. "Joe you need to get a life," he told him. "I think you feel more comfortable around dead people than live ones."

"Hey Joseph! What are you doing, chasing ambulances now? Don't you have enough cases to keep you busy? You have to follow them to the morgue now?"

"Just curious to know how this one died." Joseph answered.

"I hope it's not another friend of yours," Joe said.

"No, but I knew her. I questioned her a year ago about a murder."

"Ok, just give me a few minutes and we'll see how it was done. But just offhand, I bet she OD'd on crack or something. If that's the case we'll have to wait until we get the tox screen back. Hey, why don't you go to the lobby and get us a coke from the machine. That'll give me time to look her over."

"Ok."

Joe already an idea about the death of the girl by the time Joseph got back. He took a big swig on the bottle of coke before he said anything. "You see these little broken vessels around her eyes, they're called petechia, and the slight blue tint around the mouth, that shows me that her oxygen was cut off. I'd say without going any further that she was murdered by suffocation. We may very well find crack in her system, but see the little broken vessels around the nose, and the white powder up in her nostril? It looks like someone forced the stuff up her nose after she was dead so we'd think that's how she died. If she had sniffed it, all traces would have been brought into the nasal canal."

"So we have another murder," Joseph said. "I guess we have our work cut out for us. Thanks Joe. And try to go home and have fun with your wife for a change." He laughed as he left the room.

Well it looked like it would be a long night. He hated being away at night, especially when Jennie was so close to delivering the baby. However, it couldn't be helped. It was his job and it went with the territory.

He headed to Bourbon Street. He knew it would be busy this time of night. The drunks were just getting started good.

Sure enough, the street was crowded with tourists walking around, peeking in doors of strip joints. Joseph saw even more demonic activity here. Actually, the sky overhead was black with demons. "They'll find a lot of warm bodies here," he thought. "Sin city—and people actually paid good money to travel here for this."

"Lord," he prayed in his mind, "watch over Jennie. Keep her safe for me. You blessed us with each other, and Father, please guard what You've put together. In Jesus' Name."

He started with the Jazz Club since that's where she had hung out when he knew her. Nothing had changed. He guessed all the places stayed the same, just got older and shabbier.

The band played a jazz piece that he had enjoyed in the past. Dave Brubeck originally recorded it, and at one time, he had it in his CD collection, since it had been one of his favorites. Now he didn't even listen to Jazz anymore. When he was home, he was content to just sit and talk to Jennie. Then of course, there were the moments when they quit talking.

He showed the bartender the picture Ray had given him. There was no doubt that she was dead in the picture.

"Sure I know her. She hangs in here all the time. Why does she look so funny in that picture?"

"They all look funny when they're dead," Joseph replied.

"What??? What happened? She was just in here last night."

"Do you know if she was a crack addict?" Joseph asked.

"Tina? Not on your life. She always talked against the stuff. Said she had better things to spend her money on."

"Was she alone last night?" Joseph asked.

"Aw, you know these strippers. They're never alone when they're off duty. Either they're with some John or some guy they're in love with."

"And which was she with last night?" He felt like he was dragging the information out of him. This guy didn't volunteer anything.

"Must have been love. He was too young to be a John. Didn't look like he had the money to buy her drinks, much less pay for anything else."

"Had he been around here before?" Joseph questioned.

"No," the bartender said. "Never saw him before last night."

"Give me some help here," Joseph said. "What did he look like? Did he speak to anyone else?"

"He just looked like an average Joe. Sandy hair, medium build. And I can't watch every customer to see who they talk to."

Joseph handed him his card. "Ok Hank, thanks for your help. Call me if you think of anything else."

Outside on the sidewalk he thought, "Boy! Getting information out of these people is like trying to wring blood out of a turnip."

He decided to go to the Golden Garter and ask around. They were busy, lots of tourists sitting in booths buying drinks for the girls who had already been on stage. He had avoided this place because it brought back memories of that last night he had seen Janna alive.

The bartender walked up and asked, "What'll it be?"

Joseph showed him the picture. "Have you ever seen this girl around here?"

"Yeah, they all make the rounds. I think she even worked here for a short time."

"Had she been in lately and was she with anyone new, someone you hadn't seen around before?" Joseph asked.

"Yeah, she came in with a sandy haired guy. They had a few drinks and she talked to one of the other girls, then they left."

"Which other girl? Is she here tonight?" Joseph asked. "Could be a lead here," he thought.

"Yeah, that's her in the booth in back with the big guy."

"Thanks," Joseph said as he headed to the back.

"Excuse me Miss," Joseph said to the girl in the booth. "I believe you know this lady?"

"Yep."

Joseph could see that she was tipsy. "Well, she was here with a sandy haired guy and the bartender said that you spoke to her before they left. Did you know the guy?"

"No, he was new. Looked kinda like a country hick if you know what I mean. Didn't seem to fit in with the Bourbon Street crowd. She just wanted to know if the owner was looking for any more dancers. She used to work here."

"Did they say where they were going?"

"No, but there was one thing about him that I noticed." She said.

"What's that?" Joseph asked.

"He had a tattoo on the back of his hand. It was a picture of the devil with a snake interwoven in the face. Gave me the creeps just to look at it."

"Thanks, you've been a big help. Here's my card. If you think of anything else, give me a call."

"Sure honey. I may just call you anyway." She smiled and winked at Joseph and he knew it was an invitation. And one he wasn't interested in.

He just smiled back and walked out of the club.

That tattoo made him think that it was related to a satanic cult. Someone wanted her dead. Maybe for revenge? "Oh God," he silently prayed. "Will this cult stuff ever end? Will we ever be safe from all the evil the devil has devised for us?"

He thought about Gary sitting on death row, awaiting his execution. He was pretty high up the ladder in that cult. He could have gotten one of the lower minions to take revenge on her. And if Gary was worrying about revenge from death row, then he and Jennie could very well be on his list. And that thought sent chills up his spine because he knew if Gary had a vendetta against them, then he just might find a way to bring it to pass.

Chapter Three

Joseph went from the Golden Garter to the Sho Bar Club. It was after one o'clock and although the strip shows had ended, there was a Jam session going on. The local talent would come here in the early morning hours and play just for their enjoyment. Most of the street people would join them just to have someplace to go strictly for fun. Strippers would head here when they got off and hang around with friends who worked at different clubs than they did.

Usually the band played jazz, as that was the popular sound with the street people. He used to hang out here to listen to jazz, but that was before Jennie. It seemed like a lot of stuff went out the window now that he had her but he didn't regret anything. She was well worth it. "And I'd rather have Jennie than all the jazz music in the world," he mused.

Joseph walked up to three girls sitting at the bar and showed them the picture of the dead girl. "Did any of you ladies know her?" He asked.

"Yeah," a redheaded girl said. "I worked with her a while back. Her name was Tina. What a shame that someone is always targeting strippers. Why don't they leave us alone? It seems like every now and then a serial killer pops out of the woodwork and starts killing women. Why don't they ever target men? Have you ever thought about that?"

Joseph laughed. "No, but you have a good point. I guess these killers just see women as the weaker sex and figure they can overpower them easier."

"Well if we all started carrying guns maybe they would leave us alone." The redhead said.

"Now you know it's against the law," Joseph said. "But I know how you feel. I'd probably buy my wife a gun if she was out every night like you ladies are."

"Sit down and have a drink with us," a brown haired girl said. "I like your style."

"Thanks," Joseph said, "but it's almost time for me to head on home and it's a little late to start drinking. Besides, I'm un-officially on duty."

The brown haired girl pouted. "You're no fun." She put out her hand to him, "My name is Brianna, and the redhead here is Ginger, the other girl is Mollie."

"Hello Brianna, Ginger and Mollie," he said as he shook hands with each one. "I'm Joseph Hall, vice cop from the First Precinct. As you probably surmised, I'm investigating the death of Tina Thompson."

"Gee," Brianna said. "I never knew her last name. Nobody around her ever uses last names. It seems funny to even hear her called by that."

"So. . ." Joseph said to get the subject back on line, "Did you girls see her lately? Was she with anyone new?"

"Yeah," the girl named Mollie said, "I saw her with a guy I hadn't seen around Bourbon Street before. I mean, not that I know everyone that comes here, but he just didn't look like the type to hang around strip joints. Looked like a farm boy. You could almost picture him riding a horse if you know what I mean. There was just a cowboy look about him."

"I saw her with a new guy one night but he didn't look like a country bumpkin," Ginger said. "This guy was handsome and looked like something of a ladies man. A real looker. He had black hair and blue eyes."

It crossed Joseph's mind that he sounded like the description he had gotten about Gary so long ago. But Gary was safely in prison so he knew it couldn't possibly be him. "Anything about this guy that was different? Any distinguishing marks like a tattoo or scar?"

"No," she replied. "The only thing that stood out about him was his good looks. And he did have pretty blue eyes. He was about as tall as you are, had a good tan."

Joseph felt like he had been catapulted back to the past again. This sounded *exactly* like the description given for Gary on that fateful night over a year ago. He didn't like it when these things seemed to come back to haunt him.

"Come on," Brianna said. "Just have one drink with us. We promise not to seduce you."

Joseph laughed. "Ok, just one." To the bartender he said, "Give me a Bourbon and water and give these girls whatever they were drinking."

"Let's go sit in that booth," Brianna said.

Joseph thought that if they were all relaxed, they might remember something worthwhile about either one of these guys, the country bumpkin and the looker. "So, did Tina leave with any of these guys when she was with them?"

"Yeah," Mollie said. "Her and the cowboy only stayed a short time then left. But the time they were here, boy, they were all over each other if you know what I mean. Like he couldn't keep his hands off of her and she was kissing him back like there was no tomorrow."

"Let me get this straight in my head," Joseph said. "Was she with the cowboy right before she disappeared, or was she with the playboy?"

Mollie looked at Ginger. "When did you see them together?" Mollie asked her.

"I think it was Friday night but I'm not sure. I come in here all the time and it's hard to pinpoint one night, or rather one morning since it's always in the morning when we come to these Jam sessions." Ginger laughed. "Night and morning all seem to run together when you've been out all night, especially if you've had a few drinks."

"I think it was Sunday morning when I saw her with the other guy, the cowboy." Mollie said. "But I'm like you; they all seem to run together. Every day is just like the last one and it's hard to remember what happened each day."

"Well girls, I don't think your information is going to help me catch the guy, but now I have a little more than I had before. At least I know there were two guys she was seen with. Did anyone notice if one of them had a tattoo on his hand?"

They all shook their heads. "I didn't get that close to him," Ginger said. "What about you girls?"

"No," they both said.

"Tina wasn't exactly our best friend," Brianna said. "You don't make too many good friends on the street. The three of us are good friends but this is really unusual. Strippers tend to be friends with the guys that hang around but not with each other. We all worked together at one time at the Watering Hole, that's how we became friends. That place—boy! You need a friend if you work there. The owner doesn't support you in anything. You have to get yourself out of your own jams. So we girls just kinda stuck together."

"Say Joseph," Ginger asked, "You got a girl or something?"

"Yeah, and she's my wife. You might know her. She has a street ministry and knows a lot of the girls in the Quarter. Her name is Jennie, it was Warden, now it's Hall."

"Say, I think I do know her," Mollie said. "Dark haired girl?"

Joseph nodded. "Dark hair and green eyes."

"I had a friend who was into drugs big time," Mollie went on, "and she prayed over her and the girl was set free from drugs. She even helped the girl leave town and get a new start in life."

"That's my Jennie," Joseph smiled. "She really gets around."

"I heard of her," Brianna said. "Seems like there was a story circulating about her a long time ago. She helped a girl get away from her pimp and he did something to her to get even. I forget exactly how the story went."

"Do you remember if it involved voodoo?" Joseph asked.

"Now that you mention it," Brianna said, "I think it did. I just can't remember the whole story. But I do remember thinking that I hoped she would be all right. It does me good to hear about someone who cares about us girls and wants to help us in spite of pimps and mobsters. She had guts."

"She sure did," Joseph said. "She still does. It's hard to keep her off the streets at night even though it's dangerous for you ladies to be out alone, as I'm sure you all know."

"That's one reason we all meet and come down here together," Ginger said. "We're not taking any chances. There's safety in numbers."

"Good for you," Joseph said. "If you stick together, you have a better chance of not becoming a next victim."

Brianna put her hand on the back of his neck. "Say Joseph, why don't you just stay and keep us company this morning. You could send the other two home in a cab and escort me home personally. I'd love for one of New Orleans' finest to escort me home."

Joseph laughed as he removed her hand. "Sorry girls, you'll just have to each take a cab home alone today. My little spitfire Cajun would have something to say about that. Besides, she's ruined me for other women. She's all I need."

"She sure is lucky," Brianna said. "I wish Mr. Joseph Hall that I had known you first. She wouldn't have had a chance with you. Even now it's not too late." She reached up and caressed his face.

He figured he'd better leave before she tried to go any further. "It's been pleasant ladies, but I need to get home to my wife. She's about to go into labor any day now and I need to stick close to her. I'm sure you understand since it's a lady thing."

"Yeah," Mollie said. "I understand that. I have a kid of my own and I remember when I was close to delivering, I sure wanted my man around to be with me when the time came."

"Come back and see us sometime Joseph Hall," Brianna said. "She won't always be close to going in labor. Come back when you have more time."

Joseph laughed and pulled out a twenty-dollar bill. "Give these ladies another drink on me," he called to the bartender as he put the money on the bar. "Good night ladies. And be sure and take a cab home. It's too dangerous to walk the streets this time of night."

"Night Joseph," they called to him as he left.

It was after two when Joseph finally got home. Now he was so keyed up he couldn't have slept if he'd tried. And Jennie had waited up for him even though he'd told her not to.

"I told you to get some rest, love." He said as he gathered her in his arms.

"I rest all day long. There's not much else I can do." She pouted. "Is that bourbon that I smell on your breath?"

"Yeah, I had one drink before I left the Sho Bar. I thought if I had a drink with these three strippers, they might relax and remember something that would help in my investigation."

"Three girls!" She exclaimed. "Joseph Hall, what were you doing with three strippers?"

He laughed. "Believe it or not, I was telling them about you. And two of them had heard about your ministry. One even remembered a story about a pimp who was going to get revenge on you and I think that's how that voodoo thing got in your bathroom that time when it made you so sick."

Jennie got quiet as she was remembering that time in the past, the time when she was dating Gary but was in love with Joseph. "Look at all the time we wasted!" She thought.

He debated whether to tell her about the dead girl or not. Maybe telling her would make her be more careful when she went out. "We had another murder victim tonight. A stripper."

"Oh no! Is it anyone we know?"

"No, I don't think you knew her. But I did. Jennie she was the girl who told me that Gary had been with Elise the night she disappeared."

"You don't think... "

"No," he cut her off. "I'm sure there's no connection. It's been a year and Gary's safely locked up in the prison on Broad Street."

"I wish they had sent him to Angola," she said. "Or any place far away from here. It gives me the creeps just knowing he's right here in the same city we're in."

"I know. It gives me the creeps too. I worry about you every moment I'm not with you."

"Don't worry my love. God will protect His warrior and keep him safe." She patted her stomach.

"I know that He has the outcome in His hands, but it's the gettin' there that bothers me," he said.

She laughed softly as she pulled his lips to hers.

The next morning Joseph stepped from the shower and grabbed for a towel but none was there. "Hon," he called, "bring me a towel."

Jennie entered the bathroom to hand him the towel and noticed something on his right shoulder. "What's that?" She asked. "I've never seen it before. It looks like a little bird."

"Yeah, that's a birthmark. I've had it since I was born according to my mother. You didn't see it before because it only darkens up when I get in a hot shower. It's there all the time but you have to really look to see it unless I've been in hot water or around some kind of heat."

She smiled. "That's the mark of the Holy Spirit that God put on you. He knew before you were even born that you would serve Him." She put her arms around him and they kissed, long and hard. She loved the feel of his muscular body against her.

"And He knew before I was born that you were the woman for me." Jokingly he added, "He also knew I'd be late for work if I don't get dressed and get out of here."

Joseph sat at his desk reading the reports that each department had filed. The ME's report was complete now and it was as he had stated. There was no cocaine in her system, only in her nostril. "Strange," he thought, "that someone would go through all the trouble of making it look like she OD'd. We find dead bodies all the time. Why try to hide the real facts of this particular one?" This brought uneasiness to his spirit. He was too connected to this one, and anything out of the ordinary didn't sit well on him.

He continued to read the report. Suffocation was given as the cause of death, and reading further down the report he noticed something that sent chills down his spine. "On the victim's back," he read, "were several small cuts appearing as little upside down crosses."

"So it is related to Satanism," he thought. "But it could be a different cult, why would it have to be the same one, the same group as it was that last time?"

He knew that Gary was still behind bars but he also knew that Gary hadn't been the only one around here that was in that cult. No telling how many others, and how high up, that weren't caught. After all, if the Police Commissioner was involved, there may have been other officials in it. And no telling just how high up it went.

He struck out again when he questioned prospective witnesses, so he figured he might as well go home. He was tired anyway from being out so late last night. His mind kept dwelling on the dead stripper. "Did it have a connection?" He wondered. "Did that satanic cult have so long an arm that it was still reaching out to victims? Was Gary controlling things even from death row?"

Jennie met him at the door. "I've missed you so much," she said, as she threw her arms around him. "It's so lonely being confined to this apartment."

"I know love, but for now it's best. Once you have the baby you can go back to your busy life, but it's too risky out there with all the evil that would like to see you dead. Demons can't stand us because they know we're using the power of God to cast them out of their comfy homes."

When he had settled down in an easy chair, she sat on his lap. "Joseph, you never talk about your father. I don't want to press you into talking if you don't want to. I'm just curious about him. I want to know every little detail about the man I love."

"Ok Jen," he sighed. "Let's get it over with and then I don't want to ever mention him again. My father is the Mafia crime boss, Michael Rossi."

"What???" She asked in amazement. "But the different name..."

"My mother had our names legally changed when she divorced him. It wasn't until I was grown that I found out from a relative when I questioned her about him. Then it all made sense, my mom becoming an alcoholic and all, why she would never mention him. My Aunt said that she really loved him but couldn't live with his lifestyle."

"But you were six. You must have known your real name at the time, before she changed it."

"Yeah, I knew it but she said when people got divorced the children took on the mother's maiden name. So I just accepted it and didn't think any more of it. I guess over the years I just forgot about it."

"My poor baby," she murmured as she clung to him. I'm so thankful that God gave us to each other. Our past wasn't too great but our future will be wonderful."

As Jennie stood up, she felt herself being thrown across the room. She put her hands on her stomach to protect the baby as much as possible. Before Joseph could run to her, a huge demon grabbed him and flung him in the other direction. These were strong, stronger than any they had encountered in the past. One stood by Jennie as the other faced Joseph.

"Listen human," the demon spoke to Joseph, "she will not carry that baby. I will not allow another human to come to earth as a deliverer."

"In Jesus' Name I command you to leave," Joseph shouted. I break your assignment against us in Jesus' Name and you have to leave here now."

The big demon hesitated only a second before leaving. "There will be others, stronger than I." With that, he left.

Joseph ran to Jennie as she lay there moaning. Blood was spurting from a vessel near her temple. Joseph grabbed the phone and called 911 as he applied pressure to the wound.

"Jennie, speak to me my love. Oh my love, are you ok?"

She felt herself slipping into darkness as she passed out.

"Oh God," Joseph cried. "Don't let anything happen to her. Please God." He crushed her to his chest as if his life could flow into her. There was blood everywhere and Joseph felt himself getting faint from seeing her life's blood all over the floor.

It seemed forever but the ambulance finally arrived and loaded Jennie into the back, Joseph right by her side. There was no one and nothing that would have kept him out of the ambulance. The EMT's tried to but he showed them his badge and said, "Police business."

"Well ok," one EMT said, "but we're not responsible if you get hurt. We go pretty fast and sometimes the ride's not that smooth. It's against the rules, you know."

"I know, I know," he answered. "I'll take full responsibility."

The doctor was concerned about the baby as well as the cut on her temple. He stitched it up and dressed it but he already had a call in for an obstetrician to make sure the baby was ok.

When he arrived, they did an Ultra Sound, and then hooked her up to a fetal monitor to watch for abnormal heart rates. "She'll have to stay in a room for the night," he told Joseph. "We need to monitor her for a while, especially since she's slipping in and out of consciousness. We'll do an x-ray to see if there's a concussion. More than likely there is."

The portable x-ray machine arrived and they took pictures of her head. It revealed a tiny crack in the skull. They took her to a room and when Joseph started to go in, a nurse stopped him. "Sir, you won't be able to stay in the room with her."

He pulled his badge out again. "Listen, there's a murder investigation going on and she's a witness. I can't leave her alone for fear the killers will try again."

"Yes sir. I'll make sure everyone on the staff knows you're here on official police business."

He smiled inwardly. There was a positive side to being a cop. And he didn't exactly lie, just changed the story a little. He had to stay and make sure those demons didn't come back to finish the job.

The nurse left and Joseph pulled a chair next to her bed. He took her small hand in his and prayed. He stayed there a long time with his head bowed, speaking to the Lord. He raised his head when he saw a bright light come into the room. It was the same light he had seen on another occasion—that unearthly light that could only come from the presence of something Holy—something from Heaven.

The angel stood at least nine feet tall. Joseph stood up and faced him, completely awed by his presence. "You are serving the Lord well Joseph. There are some trials ahead, but you must stand strong and prove yourself faithful. God is with you in all you do. Don't stray to the left or to the right for you are on the correct path. And you will be the one to help stop the evil."

Just as suddenly as he appeared, he was gone. Joseph had no idea what he meant. He wondered why these guys always left you guessing when they were gone. He wished the angel had said something about Jennie and the baby.

Jennie stirred and opened her eyes. She didn't know where she was and fear came over her like a tangible thing, crawling all over her body. She gave a small moan and Joseph quickly took her in his arms. She pulled back from him and the look in her eyes was like a wounded fawn. He loved her more in that minute than he had ever loved her before.

"Jennie, Jennie, I was so worried about you." He said.

"Who are you?" She questioned.

"Oh God Jennie, don't you know me? It's Joseph, your husband."

She shook her head from side to side. "Where am I?" She asked. "How did I get here? Who am I?"

"Its ok love, you're in the hospital. You took a fall and hit your head."

"Why can't I remember anything?" She cried in anguish. "What has happened to me?" She noticed her large stomach and the fetal monitor straps. "What is this? Am I pregnant?"

Joseph pushed the buzzer to call the nurse. When she arrived, he fired questions at her. "Why can't she remember anything? What's wrong with her? Where's the doctor?"

"Whoa, Mr. Hall, one thing at a time. What are you talking about?" The nurse asked.

"She can't remember who she is, or who I am, or even the baby."

"Just calm down," the nurse said. "I'll call the doctor. He'll give you some answers."

Jennie still just sat there as if frozen, that look of fear in her eyes. Joseph couldn't understand why this was happening. The angel just implied that everything would be all right, that he was on the right path. He tried to take her hand but she drew back from him and suddenly it was Christmas all over again, and he was that little seven-year-old boy who didn't get anything that Christmas. Everyone had let him down, even Santa Claus. He felt that gut wrenching pain that he had felt then, and wondered if anything would ever be all right again.

"Amnesia," the doctor said. "It could just be temporary, but there's no way to know. Only time will tell. You'll just have to be patient with her Mr. Hall."

"But she doesn't even remember our baby!" Joseph cried out in anguish.

"I know. But there's nothing either one of us can do. Time is the healer."

Joseph took Jennie home the next day, since there was nothing further the doctor could do for her. He suggested that Joseph expose her to everything normal in their life and perhaps something would jog her memory.

She accepted what he told her, that she had amnesia and that she was his wife. However, nothing he said or did wiped that look out of her eyes. That look of fear. And it broke his heart every time he looked in her eyes.

Jennie herself was having a hard time dealing with this. She felt so alone, like she was living with a stranger. Her thoughts went round and round in her head like a hamster on a wheel. What else could she think about? She didn't know anything else. It was all a blank—a big fat nothing.

She was glad that if she had to have a husband he was at least a good-looking one. But she wanted to remember the love, remember their wedding, anything that would connect her to him.

And what about the child she carried? Joseph told her they were going to name him Joshua, and it broke her heart that she couldn't remember all the plans they made together; couldn't even remember her own baby. It was as if time didn't exist before now. Like there was nothing in the past, no family, no love, nothing. And she lived in fear, a fear that gripped her continuously. A fear that nothing would erase, and no one could help her get away from the fear. This man Joseph kept telling her that he loved her. But even he couldn't help her.

Joseph wanted so badly to take her in his arms but he didn't want to scare her any more than she already was. He was afraid to go to work and leave her alone so he hired a woman to come in and stay with her during the day. And he prayed continually for her recovery.

"Please God, return my Jennie to me. Let her remember me, remember our love together, remember our child."

The next night she had the dream again. The one where she was surrounded by evil faces as they danced in a circle around her. She tossed and turned in her sleep, every now and then letting out an audible sob. She screamed and sat straight up in bed, nightgown wet with sweat. Joseph grabbed her and held her to his chest. She fought feebly to get away.

"It's ok Jen, I'm here and you're safe. I won't ever let anything hurt you."

She relaxed against his chest. He couldn't help himself, his lips found hers and he was lost. He felt consumed by her, an ecstasy he remembered, a passion he had missed. He continued kissing her, nuzzling her neck, speaking love words in her ear.

She responded to his passion with a passion of her own that surprised her. She was allowing this stranger to kiss her passionately and not only that, she was kissing him back just as passionately. She didn't remember the love, the feelings from the past, and this passion surprised her. She had never to her knowledge, kissed anyone like this but she gloried in it. Their passion consumed them both.

Long after Joseph was sleeping, Jennie lay awake and tried to remember: to remember the love, to remember her baby, to remember anything. But it was just blackness. She softly cried herself to sleep.

Chapter Four

Joseph knew that this whole situation was even harder on Jennie than it was on him. His heart went out to her. He couldn't even begin to imagine not having any past, any memories. Of course, the only memories from the past that he was concerned with were the memories of her—of how she had invaded his life—consumed him.

"Maybe when she has the baby it will jar her memory back," he thought as he read the newspaper. He was sitting at his desk in the precinct, unable to focus on anything but her and their problems. He remembered their passion last night and flushed. He couldn't seem to think of anything else all morning.

They were in the Mardi Gras season and he read that the parade of Endymion was next week. "Maybe taking her to the parade will trigger a memory. After all, she's from here and had attended parades in the past. Maybe I could even get some tickets for Endymion's Ball. Maybe a night of fun and relaxation would help her. Maybe, maybe, maybe... That's all I seem to think lately. I just don't see how anything's going to help her."

Mardi Gras started a long time ago, and at different times in different places other than New Orleans. Early Christians only performed baptisms on Easter Sunday. Therefore, people would fast and pray before being baptized, and that tradition became Lent in the Catholic Church. Mardi Gras Day was on Tuesday because it was the day before Ash Wednesday, and the beginning of Lent.

Before a period of prayer and fasting, people wanted to celebrate. Therefore, Fat Tuesday. Christianity spread, and Lent spread along with it.

In New Orleans when interest had waned and Mardi Gras wasn't generating the tourists it had previously attracted, Endymion parade and ball was created. Endymion brought young people back to a dwindling Carnival time, by changing the sound and feel of Mardi Gras. Well-known stars of stage and screen were recruited as King of Endymion, and Carnival suddenly had glitter and flash. The krewe also brought an element of variety to the celebration that had been absent.

But Joseph wasn't interested in the history of Endymion or Mardi Gras. He was only interested in getting his wife back. He called Lois Miller to see if she could help.

"Hi Lois, this is Joseph."

"Oh Joseph, I'm so sorry about Jennie's accident. How is she doing?"

"She's not doing well at all, Lois. In fact, she has amnesia and, really Lois, I'm at a loss as to what to do to help her remember. The doctor said to try different things to jog her memory. But she doesn't even remember me and the baby."

"Oh no!" She exclaimed. She was horrified. She remembered so well the love between them, and how she knew they were meant for each other. "Can I help? Maybe if you bring her to the Plantation she might remember something."

"Well I thought I might take her to Endymion's Ball and parade. Anyway, she's been cooped up so long she needs to get out and have some fun. You wouldn't by any chance have tickets to the Ball?"

"I sure would and I'll send them to your house with my driver."

"Thanks Lois. I'll keep in touch."

Joseph was pleased with her progress. She still didn't remember anything, but at least she would say his name. She wouldn't even do that in the beginning and it took a lot of effort to get her to say it. She still didn't mention the child or seem to have an interest in him, but in time maybe…He couldn't even bear to think about the future, only one day at a time.

"Oh Jennie," he groaned under his breath. "I miss you so much." The cold stranger who sat in his house was not his beloved, his wife. She was a beautiful shell, a false imitation of the real thing.

He took her shopping for a gown for the Endymion Ball and since she showed no interest, he chose one for her. He helped her try it on in the dressing room. It was a gorgeous emerald silk with a princess bodice. It was gathered under the breast and draped down across her large stomach; complementing it instead of emphasizing it. His breath caught in his throat when he saw her in it. She was more beautiful than ever. In spite of not remembering anything, being with child had produced an inner glow that seemed to radiate out of her. Almost a holy thing.

"You look stunning Jennie. You'll be the envy of the ball."

It didn't mean anything to her. She just wanted her life back—to remember. "Will that please you Joseph?" She asked without emotion.

"I only want you happy Jennie. I just want to see a smile on your face once more, to hear your laughter fill our home, to hear you say, 'Joseph I love you'."

"If that will make you happy, Joseph I..."

"No!" He cut her off. "I don't want you to say it because I wanta hear it. I want you to say it because you mean it. Oh Jennie..." He took her in his arms and tenderly held her. "The forces of hell couldn't stop our love for each other in the past; we can't let them win now. I'll win your love again even if you never remember me. I'll make you love me again." He kissed her long and tenderly. There was no passion involved, just a tenderness for his beloved.

The night before the parade and Ball Jennie had the dream again. This should have been a warning to Joseph, but he was so wrapped up in what they used to be that he didn't pay much attention to the present. Again, she woke up screaming and he comforted her like a little child. She slept cradled in his arms all night.

As she dressed for the Ball, she thought about Joseph. She could say his name now, and she felt a feeling for him that she didn't recognize. He was all she knew in this new lifetime. She had to cling to him because she had nothing else. Sometimes in quiet moments, she felt a flicker of an emotion that she couldn't identify. It was a good feeling, a warm feeling. But it would soon pass and she thought no more about it.

Joseph watched her as she dressed. She was a vision of loveliness and as she applied lipstick to her full lips, he had a hard time controlling the urge to take her in his arms and smother her with kisses.

She had her hair piled high on her head and wore it in the fashion of the Civil War period, making her look older, more mature.

He was dressed as a Confederate officer and looked dashing. The yellow silk sash around his waist added to his costume, making him very handsome indeed. Jennie looked at him as he dressed and wished with all of her heart that she could remember their love together. That she could feel something, anything. Anything except this empty vortex, this nothingness. Sometimes she got a headache just straining to stretch her mind, her thoughts, to bring back a memory of something.

Joseph would talk to her and tell her things about their past together, but not even a flicker of remembrance would come to her. It was all just words. Nothing seemed to bring the pictures into her mind that would go with the words he spoke.

He had decided to pass up the parade and just take her to the Ball. The streets were filled with boisterous people and he didn't want her to get hurt. He knew the demonic forces would be out tonight doing their dirty deeds, so he prayed and asked God to send a legion of angels to guard them.

He feared for her safety still when it came to nighttime. Darkness—that's when the demons would be out in full force. And he knew that they would never give up trying to harm him or Jennie. She might not remember that she was God's Anointed, His deliverer, but the demons never forgot. They would try to harm her if they got a chance, but he would make sure that she was never out of his sight. He would protect his love even from the powers of darkness, the evil that was in their world.

They arrived late and the place was packed with revelers, all in costumes or formal attire. The room was decorated in purple and gold streamers, the colors for Mardi Gras. Joseph knew that most would be drunk before very long. People in New Orleans celebrating the Mardi Gras season didn't need an excuse to drink. It seemed to go with the occasion.

The band played a slow song and couples swayed together all over the room. Most wore masks and Jennie had on a black mask that just hid her eyes. It had come with the dress and there was a small green rose embroidered on it. Joseph chose not to wear one.

They danced and he held her tightly. It brought to his remembrance another dance so long ago when he was half-drunk, and bold enough to kiss her until he felt weak. He remembered how she looked that night, how she pressed even closer into him as he kissed her neck, then her shoulder. That was before he knew she was in love with him and they were always at odds with each other. Yet there were those moments indelibly etched in his mind—those sweet stolen kisses—that all consuming passion.

He kissed her on the neck, trying to arouse a spark in her, a spark that would ignite the lost passion, the lost memories. And for a moment, he thought he had succeeded. She looked him in the eye and he could see the old fire there, just for an instant.

"Oh my precious Jennie," he groaned, his face lost in her hair. "Come back to me Jennie."

"Joseph," she said softly, and he felt the old Jennie come back for a moment, but then the band started playing a fast song and the revelers went wild. They formed a long train, each one holding on to the person in front of them, and somehow Jennie got separated from Joseph. He called frantically for her as he tried to spot her in the crowd. He tried to break through the human chain but he couldn't get through.

Jennie was pulled and pushed, until she found herself out on the patio. The cool night air hit her face and she shivered, more from a premonition of something than from the coolness of the air. She turned and found that partygoers in masks surrounded her. And she realized that she was trapped in the very nightmare that had haunted her sleep. There was a variety of faces, some animal, some monster and they danced and circled around her. And once she started screaming, she couldn't stop. She felt herself falling, that familiar blackness coming over her. And before she succumbed to the darkness, she felt hands lifting her, carrying her away from the evil masks. She tried to call Joseph's name, but the darkness was upon her.

Joseph was frantic, and guessed that he had gone a little crazy. He searched for her until everyone was gone from the building, and he found a single black mask lying on the ground. There was a small green rose embroidered on it.

Chapter Five

Joseph went to the Precinct to report that his wife was missing, possibly kidnapped. Captain Parmeter was there, which was unusual so late in the night.

"Joseph, you must have read my mind. You're the very person I wanted to see." He ignored the costume. This time of year in New Orleans it was commonplace to see people in costumes.

Joseph saw a tightness in his face, a look he had never seen before on the captain and his heart seemed to stop beating. Whatever was wrong he knew that it involved him and Jennie.

"Captain, Jennie's missing. She disappeared at the ball and I've been frantic." He ran his hands through his hair nervously, tears in his eyes.

The captain turned ashen and sat down in a nearby chair. "Joseph I'm afraid I've got some really bad news and it may relate to her disappearance." He paused as Joseph just stood there, barely breathing. "Gary escaped from prison today."

Joseph had never passed out in his life but he now felt blackness closing over him as he slumped to the floor. Some of the cops picked him up and put him in the holding room on a cot.

As he started to come to, he felt like he was trapped in a nightmare, and he remembered Jennie having that dream last night. "Fool," he thought, "maybe that was a warning. Oh why didn't I just lock her up in the house and keep her safe?"

"How?" He mumbled when he came to.

"Gary has lots of friends in that cult he belonged to. Some say there's a whole network of them across the city. Somebody helped him sneak into a laundry truck and escape. Cops were involved of course. He couldn't have gotten out of death row without help. There's a big investigation right now at the prison. I think I heard that he had gone to the infirmary with a cut on his arm. Probably done on purpose. From there he was taken to the laundry truck. We're getting a task force together to search for him, but son, I have to be honest with you; this network is powerful, rumored to have even big Mafia leaders in it."

Joseph felt sick. "Oh please God, send your angels to keep her and our son safe." He prayed.

Joseph would have been surprised to know that there were angels standing next to him at that very moment. "Should we ask the Father if we can help him?" One of the angels asked the other.

"No," the second one replied. "The Father has already informed me that Joseph will only become stronger in the end if we allow events to take place. He can't serve the Lord if he doesn't grow in Him and increase in faith."

"What about those over there?" He asked as he pointed to a bunch of demons in the corner of the room.

"Joseph will see into the spiritual realm and he will take care of the ones that need to be cast away when the time comes. In the meantime, we will continue to watch over them."

His Guardian Angels continued to stay by Joseph. They would not interfere but they would watch and make sure he was ok. Even though Joseph didn't see them, he suddenly felt comforted. He didn't understand it, but he trusted God to be with him and to watch over Jennie and Joshua.

Gary Braddock started out as Gary McRae. His foster father, Mr. Simpson believed in working from sun up to sun down, and even as young as four, Simpson insisted on Gary staying with him all day until he knocked off. When Gary would get tired and sleepy, Mr. Simpson would use the electric cattle prod to jolt him awake. He said it produced character and a man was never too young to carry his weight.

Gary didn't know any better and thought all kids went through this. When he got old enough to understand that he was being abused, he was too prideful to tell anyone. He suffered at old man Simpson's hands until he reached sixteen. Then he felt as if he'd had enough. By that time, he was physically working from four a.m. until time to leave for school, and then from the time he got home until suppertime at dark.

Mr. Simpson still used the cattle prod on him when he felt like Gary was not moving fast enough, or working hard enough. One day he just grabbed the cattle prod from the old man's hands and beat him with it until he was dead. Then he went into the house and beat Mrs. Simpson with a brick until she stopped yelling and he knew she was also dead. In all the years he had been with them, she had never raised her voice in his defense or treated him kindly.

Gary changed his name to Braddock and went to work for a real estate company. The owner took to Gary and even called him his nephew. He was the one who got Gary involved in satanic worship.

When Gary had to leave Minnesota and came to New Orleans, he again got involved in a satanic cult. The Police Commissioner was a good friend of the man who owned the Real Estate Company and agreed to help Gary get a job on the force.

Gary would lead the victims that were to be sacrificed to the place where they held their high mass, and the high priest would offer the sacrifice on a wooden altar that was set up.

When they had all been caught and arrested, Gary and several others were charged with murder and waited on death row for their appointed time to die. Those who turned states evidence and assisted in catching others, including high placed officials like the Police Commissioner, had received lighter sentences.

The strong arm of the well-organized cult had fingers reaching all over the city. And some of the fingers were controlled by Gary. He had made sure that the girl who told Joseph about him being with Elise had gotten her just reward, even though it took a year for his revenge to be completed. But Gary was not one to overlook anything. He saw that all the details were taken care of, all the T's crossed and the I's dotted.

And Joseph and Jennie were two of the details that he had long waited for, dreamed about day and night, anxious to take care of. But Gary knew that patience had its own reward.

Jennie was in a large bedroom and as she tried to sit up, she fell back on the bed. She thought she recognized the familiar feeling of being drugged and was surprised that she recognized or remembered anything. "Why won't they ever leave us alone?" she wondered out loud.

A voice spoke out of the darkness from the corner of the room. "Because my love, you have something we want."

His voice sounded vaguely familiar but she couldn't place it. "Who are you?" She asked.

He entered the circle of light from the small lamp on the nightstand. "It's me, Gary."

She looked intently at him but recognition didn't dawn in her eyes. "I'm sorry; I don't know who you are."

"Come on Jennie, don't play games. You know very well who I am."

"No, I don't know who you are, but what do I have that you could possibly want?"

"You got away from us last time so we couldn't sacrifice your body to my master the devil, but your son won't get away. He'll be our next sacrifice." This last he uttered in a triumphant voice.

"Please, whoever you are, please don't take my child. He's all I have left."

"What do you mean, what happened to your precious Joseph? I'd heard that you two got married."

"Yes," she said. "We got married, and now I can't even remember any of it."

"What do you mean? What's happened?"

"I hit my head and have amnesia. I can't remember anything from the past. I meant it when I said I didn't know you. If you're from my past, then you've ceased to exist."

This excited him greatly. He had wanted her to love him but Joseph always stood in the way. Maybe now..." He wouldn't let himself finish the thought. There was too much other stuff at stake. His voice softened a little, "I'm sorry Jennie, but we really have to use your baby. I have no choice."

She started crying softly. She had finally accepted the fact that she was carrying a son, and even though she didn't tell Joseph, she had come to love the child within.

His voice remained soft as he injected the drug into her. "Sleep now my love. You must rest for the labor ahead."

Gary left the room and went downstairs to meet with his host in the large living room. They were in a three-story mansion and his host was the new elder in the satanic cult.

"She's sleeping?" The other man questioned.

"Yeah, I gave her a shot. She'll sleep a long time. Don't worry, she's not going anywhere. And this time, nobody's coming to her rescue."

The other man just nodded his head. His mansion was well guarded. He had made sure nobody could get in or out.

"When will the doctor be here?" Gary asked.

"In the morning. He'll induce labor and we'll look at this so called warrior of God."

Gary couldn't keep his mind off of Jennie. He had wanted so badly in the past for her to love him, but always it was Joseph. Right now she might not remember him, but she didn't remember her love for Joseph either. He felt jubilant. He knew that something good was going to come to him at last.

Jennie was in and out of consciousness and when she slept, she dreamed of her and Joseph dancing. He held her tightly, and all the while was planting little kisses on her face. He kissed one eyelid, then the other, finally his lips found hers and time stood still. There was no one in the world but the two of them, locked in a kiss that lifted her to the portals of heaven. The kiss left her weak and she felt him scoop her up in his arms and carry her to a bed that was in the room.

But she didn't understand why he had stopped kissing her and was sticking a needle in her arm. The dream changed and suddenly Joseph was gone and she was afraid. She heard voices around her but couldn't keep her mind focused on what they were saying. Something about a baby....

Before long, she started feeling pains in her stomach, long contractions that seemed to last forever. When one finally subsided, another took its place shortly. She tried to focus on those around her bed but she could only focus on the sharp pains coming at regular intervals.

She felt the baby moving in her and tried to tighten her stomach to keep him there. She didn't want them to take him from her. "Joseph," she inwardly cried, "you said you'd keep us safe. Oh Joseph, where are you?"

She murmured something she hadn't said in a long time, something lost in her past. "In Jesus' Name, in Jesus' Name, I command the darkness to depart."

Those around the bed heard what she said and one of them said, "Shut her up. Give her another shot."

"No," the doctor said. "We need her to push. Come on Jennie, push, get him out."

Jennie didn't want to push but the feeling was too strong on her. She gave a big push and the baby was born. She felt a needle prick her arm and before sleep overtook her, she saw a small baby being held by a stranger, and she heard his cry. A sound she would never forget.

The demons in the room had taken in all that transpired. "It won't be long now," one of them said, "and we'll see an end of this new warrior of God."

"Yes," another one answered. "And we'll make sure these humans take care of the girl too. It's already been arranged for Joseph. He'll get what's coming to him also."

They didn't see the angels standing by listening and watching all that transpired. One of the angels spoke to another one nearby, "Are they right? Are they going to get rid of God's warrior as well as Jennie and Joseph?"

"The Father has it all planned out. These fallen angels never know the outcome. So just watch and see what happens," the other angel answered.

Chapter Six

Joseph had never felt so frustrated in his life. He was working with the task force because he had to be doing something. They had the room set up with corkboards all around to put up reported sightings and clues with pushpins.

The news was giving it good coverage and a few people had called in with leads that went nowhere. In a city as big as New Orleans, one could disappear, never to be seen again. Joseph knew this well and felt the futility of it all. All he could think was "Please God, please God, please God." He couldn't even pray any further than that. His mind couldn't latch on to a prayer other than that.

"Where is she?" He wondered. "Is she still alive? I would know if something had happened to her, if she were dead." Then he remembered that they only sacrificed on new moon nights and grabbed a calendar. There was not another new moon for two nights. "Thank God." He murmured.

Jennie awoke in the same bedroom she had been in earlier. She had on a clean nightgown and as she felt her stomach, she knew it hadn't been a dream. Her baby was gone. She sobbed quietly, heart-wrenching sobs it seemed to Gary who sat in the dark and watched her. She was so beautiful, so innocent. He didn't know if he could let her go again. It was his job to kill her and dispose of the body, but he wasn't sure if he could do it or not. He just continued to watch her, and to think—he needed to think.

A housekeeper had carried the baby upstairs and she bathed him in warm water as he screamed and kicked his feet. The owner of the mansion walked into the room as he was being bathed, and looked down at him. He was surprised to see a birthmark on his right shoulder. It looked like a little bird. He turned abruptly and left the room.

"Send for Chavez," he told his henchman downstairs. "Tell him to get over here now."

"Ok boss."

Michael Rossi had come a long way from the days when he was just a med student at Tulane University. In med school, he had his whole life ahead of him and life seemed rosy at the time.

He was old now, but he still remembered the fire of his youth; he remembered the day he first saw her. She was walking across campus, the sunlight reflected off her golden hair; a shimmering radiance that seemed to cover her hair like a veil.

She was wearing a blue and white plaid skirt with a white blouse that had a tiny rounded collar trimmed in lace. She wore saddle oxford shoes, black and white. He was amazed that after all these years he still remembered what she had on that day.

He turned to his friend Mo and said, "Hey Mo, I'll give you five dollars if you'll bump into her and knock her books on the ground."

Mo, a not too bright fellow, said, "Why should I do that? She ain't done nothing to me."

Mo was in college on a football scholarship. He wasn't exactly a whiz with education, but great passing a football.

"Look Mo, after you knock them out of her hands, I'll come up and pick them up. That way I can get to meet her."

"Oh! Ok."

Mo did as he was paid to do and Michael rushed over to pick up her books. "Hello, I'm Michael Rossi. I didn't catch your name."

She laughed a soft throaty laugh. "I guess it's because I didn't give it." She started to walk away.

"Wait a minute," Michael quickly said. "I paid him five dollars to bump into you and you won't even tell me your name?"

She laughed again. "Did you really do that?"

"I sure did. When I saw the most beautiful girl on campus, I knew I had to meet you. After all, how can you become my wife if I don't get an introduction?"

She liked his brassy assertiveness. "I'm Deborah Hall, first year med student. So. . . Michael Rossi, did you get your money's worth?"

He wouldn't give her hand up. "I sure did. But I didn't get your phone number."

"I don't even know you, why should I give my number out to a stranger?"

"Because I told you, I'm your future husband. I guess that gives me a right to have your phone number."

She laughed again. Her whole face lit up when she laughed. "Vernon 3245. And I have to get to class."

Michael Rossi knew that he was in love. All it took was that one look at her and he was lost. He knew that she was the woman for him and he didn't need to look any further. They quickly became a couple around all the hangouts on campus. Whenever they were seen together, he was always holding her hand. They shared their dreams. They would both become doctors and help people get well. That was their goal; to have an office with a sign over the door, Michael Rossi, MD, and Deborah Rossi, MD.

But dreams are sometimes far from reality. He remembered that fateful day.

"Michael, I think I'm pregnant." She was crying.

He took her in his arms. "Don't worry honey, it'll be ok." He didn't know what else to say. But he wondered if their dreams would ever come true now.

They slipped over to Mississippi one night and got married. Their friends, Bob and Janet, were their witnesses.

He didn't care that they had to put some of their dreams on hold. She couldn't finish college now, but he loved her so much, they would be ok. He would support her and she would raise their kids. She was disappointed but like him, very much in love.

Michael took a part time job to pay the rent on the tiny apartment they found off campus. There was barely room to walk around, but he kept reassuring her that things would get better.

Deborah's family had disowned her so they were no help, and Michael didn't have a family really, just a maiden aunt who didn't have much herself. He became the sole breadwinner and for a while, they did all right. But once the baby arrived, expenses started coming at them faster than he could pay the bills.

The baby boy, Joseph, was his pride and joy. He felt like life was complete. Every man needed a son to feel like life was worthwhile, to have a legacy to carry on the name. But he hadn't counted on all the medical bills, all special medicines that the new baby required. Soon he was dropping classes, working more than he was going to school. Still it was hard to make ends meet.

But Michael never felt trapped. He would do whatever it took to take care of his wife and son. He loved them so much it awed him at times.

It was inevitable that he would eventually drop out of school. A friend introduced him to NeNe Giovanni. And NeNe took a liking to him and offered him a job as a numbers runner. With this job he could make enough to take care of the bills, and have some left over. They could actually enjoy life a little.

He accepted it and saw the last of Tulane University. "Maybe I'll be able to go back next year," he told himself. But even as he thought it, he knew he'd never be a doctor.

Deborah was very upset when he took the job with NeNe. He was a well-known Mafia leader in New Orleans, and Deborah didn't want him associated with someone like that. She wanted their son to be raised respectably. "Please Michael, don't take that job. There's bound to be something else out there for you."

"Yeah," he answered, "there are lots of jobs out there. I could dig ditches; maybe get on at the University bookstore making twenty cents an hour. But I want more than just getting by. I want us to have something. That's why I wanted to be a doctor in the first place. And for now, this is the best there is for me."

She knew enough not to continue arguing with him. Once his mind was made up, that was that. So after a while she accepted it and never said any more about him working for NeNe.

And they had their love to keep them together. That, and their son Joseph. He was a special little boy right from the beginning. He hardly ever fussed and cried, only when something hurt him. He smiled and laughed whenever Mom or Dad talked to him. So life wasn't bad after all.

Michael Rossi was jolted out of his memory lane wanderings when Chavez entered the room.

"You sent for me boss?"

Chavez was a big Italian fellow who had worked for Michael for over twenty-five years. He was the right hand man. Michael could confide anything to him and know that his loyalty was intact, that he would always be there for Michael, and that he would never tell a soul whatever Michael told him.

"I have a job for you, and it has to be done tonight." Michael said.

Chavez just nodded his head. Whatever it was, he would get the job done.

"I need you to take one good man with you, one you trust completely. And I want you to go to Charity Hospital and steal a newborn baby boy. A white baby with light hair. If there's none in the nursery there, go to other hospitals until you find one."

The big guy just nodded again. He didn't have to ask questions. If Michael Rossi wanted him to steal a baby, that's what he would do.

Chavez left and Michael went upstairs to the bedroom where the baby lay. He gently picked him up and cradled him to his chest. He sat in a nearby rocker and gently cooed to the baby, his first grandson.

Michael's mind went back to those years long ago when Joseph was that little baby. He and Deborah had a good life together. But ambition can ruin a good man in a heartbeat. NeNe was not satisfied for him to remain in the position he held. NeNe had taken a liking to Michael. He saw something in this young man, a steely resolve that would carry him through many trials.

Before long Michael was second in command. He was in the big time. He carried a gun and swaggered with the best. Deborah cried and pleaded with him to leave the mob, but he didn't know any place else he could make this kind of money, get this kind of respect.

Deborah loved him with all of her heart. She knew she could never love another man. But she knew she couldn't live as a mob wife. He never spoke about what his job was exactly, but she knew that it involved murder, prostitution, gunrunning, and drugs.

He came home one day when Joseph was six, and she stood in the living room with her bags packed. He grabbed her and pulled her into his arms. "You can't leave me Deborah. My life won't be complete without you. Just give me a chance. It'll get better, I promise you."

"I can't see my son raised to be the next mob boss. I love you with all my heart Michael. But I can't live like this any longer."

He let her walk out and didn't even protest when he was served with divorce papers. He loved her enough to let her go. He never attempted to see her or his son again.

And years later when NeNe died, Michael Rossi became the new Mafia leader of the New Orleans mob. Also known as La Cosa Nostra. He had learned the business from the ground up, had become like a son to NeNe. There was nobody else who could fill his shoes. In time he branched out and his organization was now spread over several states.

He brought himself back to the present and focused on his grandson. He looked just like Joseph when Joseph was a newborn. He had the same dimples, the same blue eyes and blonde hair, the same birthmark. He wondered briefly how Joseph was doing. He knew that he could find out everything about him if he wanted to, but he didn't want to know because it hurt to be involved with the son he loved and lost.

But life had made it up to him by dropping his very own grandson right in his lap. Almost like he had been handed a page from the past with a new beginning on it.

Chapter Seven

Michael Rossi was new to this cult stuff. He was a good friend of the ex-commissioner and had let the commissioner convince him to get involved. That's the only reason he allowed Gary to hide out in his home.

He thought about his grandson and felt a warm feeling. He had failed his son but he wouldn't make that mistake with his grandson. In a small way, maybe he could make up to Deborah for the pain he had caused her. He took her death hard but he took her life even harder. He knew that he was the reason she had started drinking, but there was nothing he could do to help her. The deed was done. He was high up in Mafia business by that time. There was no way out—no chance to become anything else.

He sent for Gary and poured them a drink before speaking. "I want the woman taken away from here but I don't want her killed," he told Gary.

"What?" Gary asked, surprised.

"You heard me. I have my reasons but if you can't handle it then I'll get my man to take care of it."

"No, I can take care of it," Gary said.

Michael Rossi continued, "I'll set you up in an apartment in the French Quarter. People can blend in there and no one's the wiser. Just don't hurt the woman."

Gary was shocked. This is exactly what he wanted and here it had dropped right in his lap. He wanted a chance to win Jennie's love. He'd even give up his membership this time in the cult if he had to. She was worth it. And he didn't want to ever let her go again. He remembered her kiss and was anxious to take her in his arms again. He wondered briefly if amnesia had changed her.

Gary would have been shocked to see all the black figures hanging around him and Michael Rossi. They were all over the mansion. Many were all over him. And he would have denied it if someone had told him. The air above the mansion grounds was one big black cloud.

Jennie was trapped in her drug-induced nightmare. She dreamed about Joseph over and over. They were at a dance and he was kissing her, and that's what she wanted him to do. She was where she belonged, in his arms. When she had a few lucid moments, she seemed to remember things, like riding horses with Joseph, sitting in a room and talking to him. She even remembered that portraits of stuffy men lined the walls. When she thought about him, she felt a warm glow.

She saw these black clad figures walking around, sometimes right behind Gary, almost like his shadow, sometimes she saw them all over him. She wondered about them, who they were, why no one mentioned them. But she figured they were by products of the drugs flowing freely in her system.

Gary told the housekeeper to dress Jennie with the clothes that were provided for her. She was still too groggy to walk, so a wheel chair was brought in, and they put her in a van to transport her to the new location. Gary continuously watched her, and had she not been drugged, it would have made her very nervous.

He got her settled in the apartment, still keeping her drugged. But he was giving smaller doses and she woke up more frequently. She was beginning to have images cross her mind, forgotten memories. And Joseph was first and foremost in her returning memories. She still couldn't latch onto anything in sequence. Just images flashing like a power point presentation.

Joseph sunk deeper and deeper into depression. The baby would have been born by now and in spite of the angels' words, Joseph didn't see how Joshua could be alive. And Jennie... "Oh my love," he thought, "are you still alive? Where are you my darling? Do you remember me, do you remember our love?" All these questions nagged at him constantly.

Michael sat in the room that had been turned into a nursery. He came here daily to see the child. He had hired a nanny to take care of him but he was beginning to have some grave concerns. He was already approaching sixty. Who would care for the boy if something happened to him? There were some decisions that had to be made.

The angels watched the whole scene that was unfolding. "Things are going as planned," one of the angels said to the other. "The baby is safe and so is God's anointed one. She will not be harmed in spite of Lucifer's plans. Should we tell Joseph the news?"

"No, it is the Father's plan to allow this in his life. He will grow stronger through this. And he will have more faith in the end."

Jennie was starting to have flashbacks about Gary but she thought it best to keep quiet about it. She didn't remember much and the little she did remember puzzled her. She thought she remembered liking him because he made her laugh. But this serious minded person who kept her drugged didn't seem to have much in common with the fun loving guy she was remembering. It was all very confusing to her.

Michael had reached a decision. He knew what he must do. Michael had located Joseph's home address, knew what he did for a living, and even knew how much money he made a week.

"Chavez, I have another job for you. Take Monkey with you and pick up a young man named Joseph. Here's the address. Make sure you frisk him. Then bring him to the warehouse."

The car was parked across the street from Joseph's apartment, but he didn't notice it when he came home. He went upstairs into the empty apartment. He had never felt so alone. He hadn't been home long when there was a knock on the door. As he opened it, two men pushed him back into the room. One of them grabbed him and frisked him, removing his gun.

"What do you want?" Joseph asked.

"Just don't worry about what we want. You'll find out soon enough." Chavez answered. He held a gun on Joseph. "Let's go."

Joseph turned quickly, knocking one of them against the wall, but the other guy responded by hitting him with the barrel of the gun. He felt woozy and would have fallen if they hadn't grabbed both arms and dragged him to the car.

The ride was short and Joseph wondered what could possibly be going on now. They pulled up at an old warehouse by the river and Joseph was told to get out. He could see demons hanging around the warehouse, the street, even on the piers behind the warehouse. The back door was open and he could see the moonlight reflected on the river. He wondered briefly if his body would end up there before the night was over.

He was told to sit in a chair that was at a square table off to the side. He waited, and while he waited, the big guy kept staring at him; almost as if he recognized him but couldn't place where he knew him from.

Actually, Chavez was amazed that Joseph was a younger version of Michael. He had been with Michael when he was young and there was no mistaking that this was his son.

Soon an older man came over to the table and Joseph recognized him from pictures he had seen.

"Do you know who I am?" The man asked.

"Yeah, Michael Rossi. I've seen your picture in the mobster's hall of fame. They don't do you justice. You look worse in person than in the picture."

"Is that all you know?" He asked.

"What else is there to know? A Mafia leader, an underground rat."

Chavez moved as if to hit Joseph for being so impertinent but Michael waved him off.

"There's one more thing to know," Michael said. "I'm your father."

"I knew that," Joseph answered. "I just don't claim you."

"So you found out." Michael said. "Did your mother tell you before she died?"

"No, she never mentioned you. She just kept her broken heart to herself until it killed her. An aunt told me. Not that I ever wanted to know anything about you."

"I loved your mother more than anything in the world. She just couldn't live with my lifestyle, and I couldn't get away from it. The kindest thing I could do was to let her go."

"Yeah, let her and her little boy go. Didn't you ever wonder about the little six year old that you turned your back on?" Joseph asked heatedly.

"Believe it or not, I did care. I cared greatly. I couldn't do anything then, but I can now." He nodded to Chavez.

Chavez went in the other room and came out holding a box; something wrapped in white cloths was inside. He laid it on the table and removed the wrapping. Joseph laid eyes on his son for the first time. There was no mistaking the little bird on his right shoulder.

Joseph picked him up gently, awed by the sight of him. He wept freely as he held Joshua to his chest. "And his mother?" He questioned.

Michael just shrugged his shoulders.

"How. . ." Joseph started to say.

Michael cut him off with, "No questions. I lost my son and I couldn't bear to see you lose yours."

He motioned to Chavez and the big man touched Joseph on the shoulder and led him out to the car. He would take him home now.

Joseph couldn't figure out how or even why, Michael Rossi, of all people, had his son. "And where is Jennie?" He wondered. "How on earth could Michael get the baby but not know where Jennie was?" It certainly was a mystery but he was so happy to have his son that nothing else mattered for the moment. Somehow he'd find Jennie, and they would be a family again. God had put them together, and they would, by His grace, continue as before.

He remembered in the past when the forces of hell had kept him and Jennie apart, had even tried to kill her, and he shuddered. He knew so well how they operated and knew that the demonic forces would do whatever they pleased if they had her.

"Please God, let her be all right. She's the only woman I'll ever love. Protect her from the forces of darkness."

Chapter Eight

Jennie was drugged less and less and looked for a plan of escape. She had no idea where she was but she wanted to get out and find Joseph. She needed him—oh God, how she needed him. Their baby was dead, and she felt empty inside. She needed Joseph to feel alive again.

She was remembering more and more, and it started coming back to her about Gary. But she had to be sly—she had to play him—she mustn't let him know. He was a killer, obviously escaped from death row. And she knew that he wouldn't hesitate to kill her.

He walked into the room and asked, "Feeling better today Jennie?"

"Yes, I feel a lot better. My mind is not as cluttered up by drugs." This last she said sarcastically.

"I know love; I've cut down on them. Need to wean you off now."

"What are your plans Gary, what do you want from me?"

"I just want you. And I want you to want me. And to that end I have somewhat of a bargaining chip. You see, I have your baby."

"What! Where? I thought he was sacrificed to the devil."

"No," he lied. "I hid him and I'm the only one who knows where he is. As long as you cooperate and don't try to get away, he'll be safe. If you should get away from me, well, I won't have any choice but to have him killed. If something happens to me, I've left orders to kill him if they don't hear from me. And if you ever tell anyone Jennie, then you will have signed his death warrant."

She ran and kneeled in front of him. "Please Gary, don't hurt him. Let me see him, just to hold him in my arms."

"In time, in time. First you must prove your faithfulness to me." He took her in his arms and kissed her long and deeply.

She felt nothing and had to force herself not to pull away. "It's for Joshua," she told herself. "And for Joseph. Somehow, I'll find a way to get back to Joseph."

Gary had heard through the grapevine that the cops had leads and were closing in on him. He contacted Michael Rossi and asked for help again. Michael told him to come to Las Vegas and he would give him a job.

Jennie felt dead inside. She didn't want to go anyplace with Gary, didn't want to leave the city she was born in, the place where Joseph and Joshua were. But if it meant keeping Joshua alive, then she would go anywhere on earth. Gary assured her that he was doing good and in safe hands. As long as they heard regularly from Gary that all was well, he would be safe. If anything happened to Gary, the little baby's life would be over. She said goodbye to her love as they drove away from the city.

Joseph rejoiced in little Joshua, he was a perfect baby; never fussed, always laughing. But after he played with him a while he would cry, remembering his beloved Jennie. He would never give up on her. He would find her and the three of them would be re-united. They were God's warriors and nothing was going to change that. He knew that if she was dead, he would feel it. And he didn't. He felt her near him with every fiber of his being. Her presence lived on in their home.

He heard the sirens but didn't pay any mind to them; not even when someone was pounding on his door. He opened it and a swat team entered, swarming everywhere. They grabbed Joseph and slammed him against the wall, then put handcuffs on him. Before he could even ask what was going on, a social worker picked Joshua up and left the apartment.

"Wha. . . What's going on, what are you doing? Where's she going with my son?"

The detective in charge strode over to Joseph. Others were searching his apartment. "Detective Ryan," he stated. "I'm in charge of this investigation."

"What investigation? What are you talking about?" Joseph look perplexed.

"The investigation of the murder of your wife, Mr. Hall."

"Murder? Jennie's dead? What are you talking about?"

"Excuse me; I should have said Mr. Rossi. You see, we know all about your mob connections with your father, Michael Rossi."

"Connections? I don't have any connections to him. Tell me about Jennie. Have you found her body?" This he said in anguish.

"No, you were very clever. But it'll turn up. They always do." Detective Ryan said. "We know all about your meeting with Michael Rossi at the warehouse, how you got your son from him. But his mother was conspicuously absent. That really makes us wonder. A newborn baby but no mother. Hmmm... Sounds suspicious to me."

"Jennie's not dead. I don't know how Michael Rossi got my son, but I know in my heart that Jennie's not dead."

"Convenient how Michael Rossi has disappeared and left you holding the bag. Joseph Hall, Rossi, whatever, I charge you with the murder of Jennie Hall. Read him his rights."

Detective Ryan abruptly left the room while Joseph was read the rights that he had so many times casually read to others.

Chapter Nine

Joseph couldn't understand why this was happening. He had lost everything, his wife, his son, his career. "It's not fair Lord," he thought. "Gary's a murderer and he's free. And here I sit in jail."

He wondered briefly if Gary had Jennie. He wouldn't put it past him. Maybe he's the one who orchestrated all of this. He wondered where Michael Rossi had disappeared to. So much to think about that it boggled the mind. "Help me Lord!" He cried. "Help me get my family back."

He wondered where his strength, his power had gone to. He sure didn't feel like he could cast out demons now. They'd probably kick his butt and send him running. "God's warrior? Ha! What a laugh!"

The trial began on Monday morning and Joseph was not prepared to face this. He had a lawyer, a man who said his name was Guy Stevens. Joseph didn't know where he came from or how he would pay him but Guy just said, "Don't worry about it. You still have friends."

Joseph sat at the table with his lawyer, facing the judge. Directly across from them to the right was the ADA and his assistant. They were the ones who would try to prosecute Joseph.

Joseph could see demons all over the courtroom. He sure hoped that God's angels were there too. He needed all the help he could get.

The Prosecutor gave his opening remarks. "We are going to prove that Joseph Hall, AKA Joseph Rossi, did directly or indirectly murder his wife, then, with the help of his father, Mafia leader Michael Rossi, took the child she was carrying. Mr. Hall was intending to skip town with the child, to an unknown destination. A destination that Mr. Rossi has already left for."

His attorney gave his opening statement, "I intend to prove that Joseph Hall did not kill his wife or anyone else, and that furthermore, the prosecutor doesn't even have a body to produce. I intend to prove that Joseph Hall loved his wife and would not have been involved in any attempt to bring harm to her."

"Your honor," Joseph's attorney said, "the defense calls Mrs. Hubert Miller to the stand."

Lois Miller stepped up to the witness stand, raised her right hand, and swore to tell the truth.

"Mrs. Miller," Guy Stevens said, "did you have the opportunity to observe Mr. Hall and his wife together?"

"Oh yes," she said. "They came to my house sometimes. In fact, they met at my house."

"And do you think that Joseph loved his wife?" He questioned.

"Definitely. They were very much in love. I saw that the first time they met. I knew they were meant for each other. I even tried to throw them together every chance I got."

"Mrs. Miller," he said abruptly, "do you think Joseph was capable of killing his wife?"

"Never," she said firmly. "He couldn't hurt a fly."

"Your witness," he said to the prosecutor.

Rob Brown was the assistant DA and knew his job well. He had only lost two cases in his career and thought that he had this one in the bag.

"Mrs. Miller," he began, "didn't Joseph Hall stay at your home sometimes?"

"Yes," she answered.

"And didn't your son turn up dead on your property?" He asked.

"Yes," she said quietly.

"And were the ones responsible for his death caught?"

"Yes, they're all in prison."

"And Joseph Hall was good friends with Gary Braddock, one of the main players in the cult ring, wasn't he?"

"I guess so," she said.

"Then how do you know that Joseph himself wasn't involved in the cult murders?"

"Oh no, not Joseph."

"So you really don't know whether Joseph was involved or not, you only think he wasn't"

"Well. . . I guess. . . No, I'm sure he wasn't." She declared.

"Can you prove it?" He asked.

"Well no, how could I do that?"

"No more questions your honor."

The trial seemed to go on and on. Joseph's head ached and he wished he were a million miles away.

Finally the ADA brought up his connection to Michael Rossi. He had called Joseph to the stand and threw grueling questions at him.

"Mr. Hall," the ADA said, "tell the court how you came to have your baby, without the woman who had recently given birth to him. And why a new mother would give up her baby and disappear."

"I don't know what happened to Jennie. I only know that Michael Rossi sent for me and gave my son to me. I don't know how he came to have him."

"And why do you think," the ADA continued, "that a well known Mafia leader would just hand a baby over to you? What's your connection to Mr. Rossi?" He continued to watch the jury box to see their reactions.

"He's my father," Joseph said wearily.

"Your father. . ." he said sarcastically. "You admit that you are the son of a Mafia leader who has people killed for any and every reason, yet you say you don't know anything about the mother of the child, how she disappeared or where she's at, even if she's alive. Where is Mr. Rossi now?" He asked abruptly.

"I don't have any idea." Joseph said.

"So you and he killed the child's mother, then he disappeared and left you holding the bag, so to speak."

Joseph was getting more and more nervous. It looked like the cards were stacked against him. Satan was doing a good job getting him convicted for a murder he didn't commit, a murder that he didn't believe had taken place.

The Prosecutor and the Defense had presented their closing statements and even to Joseph's ears, his attorney's statement seemed weak. "Lord," he prayed, "are you here? Are your angels still watching over me? I sure could use some help here today."

The jury foreman stood and read the verdict. "We find the defendant, Joseph Hall, guilty of murder."

"Guilty! They found me guilty!" He thought in amazement. "There's no dead body, no one's even sure she's dead, but they found me guilty." He was amazed at the audacity of the devil. He had played a good trick on Joseph. "Not even a body!"

He was to be sentenced next week. That was just a formality. He knew they would give him death; he knew the sentence for murder— after all, he was a cop.

"You got a visitor Hall," the guard on duty said as he popped open the jail cell. Joseph was surprised to see Guy Stevens. The trial was over. He didn't think he would see him again. Maybe now he was coming to hit him with the bill. That was so funny he would've laughed except that he felt like crying.

Guy Stevens sat on a chair in the cell and waited for the guard to leave. "Well Joseph, we did our best. This is really a weird ending for a case without a dead body. I've never heard of a murder verdict without the corpse being found."

"Yeah, well, my whole life has been pretty weird lately. This doesn't really surprise me." Joseph answered sarcastically. "In fact," he thought, "it all started getting weird after I met Jennie."

Guy stood up and looked down the hall to make sure the guard wasn't hanging around. "We have an ace in the hole, if you'd like to hear it."

"Sure, what have I got to lose now?"

"I've been retained by Michael Rossi to represent you. He paid me well, very well. And he said in case we lost, he would pay to get you out."

"What do you mean get me out? You can't change a murder verdict. That's it, it's over."

"Well he didn't exactly mean to get you out legally. Just get you out so you'll be free."

The cop in him rose up and he protested. "No way, I won't allow that."

"You'd rather walk that last mile to the death chamber?" Guy asked.

Joseph was quiet a while. He was a very principled person, but he wasn't stupid. He had run out of options. "Ok, do it. And just where am I supposed to go to not get caught?"

"Las Vegas. Michael owns the Blackjack Casino. He has a lot of pull there. Nobody will be the wiser."

Joseph nodded and Guy yelled for the guard to let him out. "I'll be in touch soon."

Joseph felt as if a new death sentence had been passed on him. "Jennie's here, somewhere, if she's alive. Now I'll never be able to find her. And what about my son? He's in a foster home. But if they gave me death, I wouldn't see either one again anyway. Live today, fight tomorrow," he thought. He'd find a way to get his family back. But for now, he had to make sure he was still alive to do it.

He didn't see the demons in his cell, taking in the whole situation. "This is not good. I thought we had him where we wanted him. The woman is gone, the child is gone, and we almost brought about his death," one of the demons said to the others. "The master will not be pleased with this."

"Ah, but he has lost his power," another demon said. "He can't even see us anymore. We really have him where we want him. And the girl. . . bah! She does not even remember that she once had power. So maybe we have accomplished more that we thought. And the child is lost to both of them so he is not one to fear anymore."

They didn't see the angels hovering around with drawn swords. "Are they right?" One of the angels asked the other. "Have God's anointed warriors lost what they had?"

"Only for now," the other angel answered. "They must hit bottom so they can be restored to their former place. They are right in the Father's plan."

They made themselves be seen to the demons and chased them away with their swords.

Guy Stevens paid him another visit. "It's all set. The guard on duty tomorrow morning has been paid. He'll hide you in a dumpster and the trash truck will take you out. They're working for us also. They'll take you to a place that's been pre-arranged, and you'll get in a white van. Then they'll take you where you'll be safe. Just be up early tomorrow and be ready. It has to happen fast."

He stood up and Joseph shook his hand. "Thanks Mr. Stevens. You've literally saved my life."

"Don't waste it Joseph. Make good use of it."

Early in the morning, Joseph was led out of the cell to the exercise yard, but on the way, the guard directed him to get into the dumpster. Shortly after he got in, he felt the rumble of the truck picking up the dumpster, and he found himself falling into the trash in the truck.

After thirty minutes or so the truck stopped and someone told him to climb out. Just as he'd been told, there was a white van parked next to the truck. He got into it and changed into the clothes they provided him.

He was on his way. He'd never been out of Louisiana before, but that's not what saddened him. He felt like he was saying goodbye to everything he had come to love in life. He thought about Jennie, how her face would light up when she saw him—how she would sit on his lap and nuzzle his neck, and work her way up to his lips. Then they would get lost in each other.

"Oh Jennie," he groaned inwardly, "I love you so much. Life won't be any good without you. If I had been sure you were dead, I'd have wanted the death sentence. I have nothing to live for if you're not in my world."

Chapter Ten

L as Vegas was a bustling city, all flash and glitter. The whole main street was nothing but Casino's. If he thought Bourbon Street was bad, this was far worse. Prostitution and drugs ran rampant here. Joseph saw something he hadn't seen lately. The sky was black with demons, far more than he had ever seen at one time. This was really sin city with a capital "S".

The men in the van took him to the back entrance of the Blackjack. "Mr. Rossi said this is best for now," they explained. "Later you'll just blend in."

Joseph didn't really care. What was there left to care about.

They took him to a penthouse on the upper floor and it was the most lavish place he had ever seen. The living room was bigger than their whole apartment had been, and there was a sliding glass door leading to a balcony overlooking the pool area. The living room was sunken and you had to go down two small steps to get to it from the foyer. The furniture looked very expensive even to Joseph's eyes. It was tastefully decorated, and he wondered if Michael had a woman living with him.

"Hello Joseph," Michael said. He wanted to offer his hand but didn't want to go too fast with Joseph.

"Hello," Joseph said without feeling. "Thanks for getting me out."

"I was glad to help out. And I want you to just rest and enjoy yourself. There's no hurry about business or anything, just relax. We'll talk later."

"So there's a payoff after all," Joseph thought. He didn't answer Michael.

Michael continued in the silence, "There's a suite below this one that's set up for you. Everything you'll possibly want or need. You'll be very comfortable there. I even got one of the boys to shop for you, but feel free to visit the shops downstairs. It's all been arranged. Just give them your name and you can get anything you want."

"You're too kind," Joseph said sarcastically. "Which name should I give them?"

Michael ignored the sarcasm and the question. "There's a bank account at the bank downstairs in your name," he went on. "You can withdraw whatever cash you need."

"Why are you doing this?" Joseph asked. "What do you expect from me in return?"

"Whether we like it or not Joseph, you're my son. And of course a father wants his son to take over the business when he's gone."

"Well you can just forget it," Joseph said hotly. "I'll never be a Mafia boss like you."

"Maybe not," Michael said, "but you're here and we both should just try to make the best of things. T Ball Mulligan will show you to your suite."

With that, he dismissed Joseph.

T Ball Mulligan, a quiet skinny man, was the one who drove the van from Louisiana. He never said much. If he did talk, you'd better pay attention because it was important. He didn't waste words. He had black hair slicked back in a style that was popular years ago, but T Ball didn't seem to mind that it wasn't in style anymore. He was from the old school. You didn't change something that suited you well.

He was as loyal to Michael as a new puppy would be. Michael had picked him up off the street, cleaned him up and gave him a good paying job as a driver. He was eternally grateful to Michael and would stick by him and do whatever it was that Michael wanted him to do. Michael Rossi inspired loyalty in those around him because he was a fair man, a good man, if you didn't count the fact that he was one of the heads of organized crime.

The suite that had been reserved for Joseph was fit for a king's son at the least. It was furnished with the best furniture money could buy. It had a sunken living room with two bedrooms off to the side. To the left was a small kitchen, and to the right was a sliding glass door leading to a patio. His suite was directly below the Penthouse suite where Michael lived. This one too, was tastefully decorated and he wondered again if there was a woman involved. He really knew nothing about Michael Rossi but guessed he would learn now that he had allowed him into his life.

Michael kept his and a few other suites for himself and good friends. He made sure they were comfortable when they stayed here. Nothing but the best would do for Michael Rossi and for his associates. This was his home away from home. When he wasn't in his mansion in New Orleans, this was his home.

He knew Joseph would turn him down right off. But give him time. He'd talk him into working with him. He wanted to teach him the business from the ground up.

Michael was making up for the past. Deborah would be pleased. She wouldn't want her son to be part of the mob, but she would be pleased that Michael had gotten him off of death row and gave him a new life.

Michael Rossi was still a power to fear. Handsome even in his late fifties, his blonde hair had become a light shade of silver. He carried himself well and the heads of the other families respected him, even while they hoped to do away with him one day and take over his business. Michael knew it, but he wasn't thinking about all of that now. He was thinking about his newfound son.

And he was so proud of Joseph, although he would never let Joseph know that he was proud of him being a cop. Joseph at least made something with his life and for that he was glad. "Of course I would prefer that he become the head of my organization, but who knows, maybe in time," he thought.

Michael didn't even give any more thought to the baby he had brought to Joseph that night so long ago. He just assumed that the mother had him and of course, he didn't remember that Jennie was the mother. In fact, he had only seen her briefly, when she stayed in his mansion. She was mostly with Gary but Michael didn't make the connection between the woman Gary had now, and the mother of the baby on that fateful day. He had told Gary not to kill her so he assumed that Gary had released her.

There were gaps in Michael's memory and there was a lot from the past that he didn't even remember. But he remembered Deborah, and he remembered his son Joseph.

Chapter Eleven

Gary seemed to thrive under the hot Las Vegas sun. His tan deepened, he grew a mustache and goatee, and was more handsome than ever. His deep blue eyes crinkled at the corners when he laughed. And he seemed to laugh often these days. He had Jennie, he had a good position in Rossi's organization, and a beautiful suite at the Blackjack Casino. It was one of the biggest gambling Casino's in Las Vegas.

Jennie herself was thriving. Her health had improved since he quit drugging her and she had accepted Gary, in fact, actually had some feelings for him. She was still his hostage, and as such, developed feelings as was common in such situations. He started making her laugh again and it felt good after such a long time of depression and emptiness.

She didn't even consider trying to escape from him. Where would she go? There was nothing left for her but Gary. She had no idea where to find Joseph. And she felt a fondness for Gary for taking care of her, for giving her a life of sorts. And she was ever mindful of Joshua.

She had gotten most of her memory back but there was still something missing and she couldn't quite put her finger on it. It just seemed like there was something else that she should know, something that she should remember. However, she didn't let it bother her. She guessed she would remember it in time also.

The demons were rejoicing because she couldn't remember that she was God's anointed, His warrior, His demon fighter. They laughed with glee at the topple of this high and mighty one who did so much damage in their ranks. They still followed her around, mostly to see what would happen in the life of this so-called warrior who had fallen from grace. They didn't fear her anymore and wondered why they ever did fear her. She was nothing, a nobody. So they watched, and rejoiced that she was not a power to fear anymore.

And the angels also watched. They knew that the Father was still in control although it looked contrary to that. But they watched, and they waited.

Motherhood had been kind to Jennie. Her body had filled out and matured, and she was more beautiful than ever. Gone was the young girl who used to live in the French Quarter, and instead a shapely, sensuous woman took her place.

Sometimes when Gary looked at her he felt lost in her presence. He just wanted to pull her to himself and smother her with kisses. He knew she only tolerated his touch, but held out hope that one day she would return his kisses with as much passion as he felt for her.

Life was good for Gary. He had Jennie all to himself and he would never let her go. He vowed it to himself, and almost daily, he vowed it to her.

His job only required that he make rounds weekly to collect from his accounts, money owed from bookies, protection money, whatever was due to be paid to the Michael Rossi Organization. And for that he made a great salary, had a free suite, and an easy life. He and Jennie shopped, swam, and gambled; whatever Gary felt like doing at the moment.

He was totally in control and he liked that heady feeling. Jennie had no say so about anything. He even picked out her clothes, and dressed her in the latest fashion; the clothes that would show off her beauty and be a reflection on him. He loved it when men turned their heads to stare at her beauty. As long as he owned her, there would be no problems. As long as she was never out of his sight.

"Get dressed Jennie. We'll do a little gambling before supper and take in a show. There's a new one starting tonight in the Casino. Wear the blue silk. We'll make every head turn when you walk into the room."

Just as Gary ordered, Jennie wore a royal blue silk gown, low cut in the bodice, draped gently across her hips. There was a slit up the front revealing long shapely legs. She was stunning and Gary was proud to walk with her through the Casino. Every male eye turned in her direction.

Her hair was piled high on her head with one long piece falling down across her cheek, caressing her soft white skin. Gone was the young girl from New Orleans. Here was a sensual woman on the arm of a handsome man.

Even early, the place was crowded with people wanting to win that fortune, that pot of gold at the end of the rainbow. Las Vegas drew all the gamblers: the professional ones and the tourists hoping to make that big score. It also drew the hustlers, the pimps, the petty crooks. These hoped to take the pot of gold from the hands of the winners. They hoped to get rich by hook or crook.

They stopped at the Roulette table and tried their luck. Number seven, black, was what Jennie chose but it came up twenty-two red. She wasn't very lucky lately.

Joseph entered the Casino and his gaze was attracted to a beautiful woman in blue silk standing by the Roulette table. His breath caught in his throat when he saw that it was Jennie. He had to hang on to the nearby slot machine to keep from falling. She was far more beautiful than he remembered and his heart was beating so fast he thought it would come out of his chest. His hands were sweaty and his mouth suddenly dry.

He had started to walk in her direction, but stopped when he saw her lean back against Gary who stood behind her. She gave a little laugh at something he said and he leaned down and showered tiny kisses on her neck and shoulder.

A murderous rage engulfed Joseph. He had worried so much about her and she was here with her lover, obviously enjoying herself and his attentions. He seriously considered shooting her. After all, they couldn't convict him twice.

He purposefully strode over to where they stood and when she saw him, she made as if to go toward him, but Gary tightened his grip around her waist. The blood drained from her face and she felt in danger of passing out. "Joseph!" She exclaimed weakly.

"Well it looks like old home week," he said sarcastically. "Just like a page from the past. Here we are again, the three of us. Looks like nothing's changed."

Jennie couldn't speak. She saw the hate in his eyes and she didn't know how to cope with it. She had never seen anything but love in Joseph's eyes for her. But she knew that at this moment, he loathed her.

Gary was quick to recover. "Well Joseph, it sure does look like a page from the past except this time I hold the ace of spades." He pulled Jennie closer to himself. She just remained stiff and unyielding.

"I'm glad to know you're doing so well Jennie," he said sarcastically. "Looks like you've got everything you could possibly want, and no responsibilities."

"Joseph, I...." she got no further. Gary had secretly pinched her as hard as he could and she got the message. She was trapped.

Joseph saw the expression in her eyes but in his rage he wouldn't allow anything to get in the way. He didn't want to see anything in her eyes, didn't want to feel anything for her. For the first time in his life he actually hated a woman. He had allowed his emotions to enter into their relationship and He had been kicked in the teeth. He would never do it again. In that instant, he became the "ice man" all over again. He had a superhuman grip on his emotions and never again would he allow himself to be hurt.

"Have a nice life." He said as he left them.

Jennie wanted to cry. She wanted to call out to him not to leave her. But Gary made his intentions plain. If she didn't play ball, he would have her child killed.

Gary wouldn't allow her to retreat to their room. He made her sit through supper and a show. She went through the motions mechanically, all the while wishing she was dead. Better to be dead than to witness the hate in Joseph's eyes. She couldn't bear to see that again. She had so many questions. "What is he doing here in Las Vegas? And if he loved me so much, why did he leave New Orleans instead of looking for me there?" She wondered.

Joseph went to the bar. "Double Bourbon," he told the bartender. He needed to wipe out the image of her. In spite of everything, he loved her more than ever. "Oh God," he thought, "why have you forsaken me? What did I do that was so bad?"

Her face stayed before him, and he cursed the day he was born. He kept seeing this new sensuous woman, this new Jennie, and even while he loathed her, he yet desired her even more than he had desired the old Jennie. He kept seeing her as she had looked tonight, and even while he hated her with everything in him, he would have given anything in the world to trade places with Gary. To be the one trailing kisses down her neck, to be the one holding her in his arms, to be the one she turned to with love in her eyes.

"What is it about her?" He wondered. "Why can't I get free of her? Why am I cursed to forever be in bondage to her face, to her body? Oh God, set me free from this." He cried passionately.

All the way here from Louisiana, he had thought of nothing but her. He would almost cry when he realized that he was leaving the place where she was. And to find her here, and with Gary of all people, he couldn't figure it out. His thoughts just kept swirling around like a whirlpool.

"And how did Gary end up here, in the very place I am?" He wondered. "This is just too weird to be a coincidence." Therefore, he figured the powers of darkness must have planned this out. And they did a really good job. The devil must be dancing with his minions to see all that Joseph was going through, to see Jennie hanging on to Gary, the devil's own.

Joseph continued drinking until he knew he would pass out if he didn't get to bed. And even in the fog of alcohol, her face was there before him. "Damn you Jennie," he thought. "You really must have put a voodoo spell on me."

Chapter Twelve

Jennie thought the night would never end. It was horrible, sitting next to Gary, him pawing her as if he owned her. And of course, that's exactly what he thought.

When they got back to their hotel suite, he backhanded her and she fell upon the bed. A large red whelp was raised on her cheek.

"Don't ever try to pull away from me and attempt to go to him. You belong to me now, and don't get any ideas. Not only will I kill your baby, but I'll kill him too. Then I won't have anything in my way. And if you don't do like I say, I'll kill you. And you know I will Jennie. So forget any thoughts about Mr. Joseph Hall that you might even entertain."

The next day even while he nursed the biggest hangover he'd ever felt, Joseph went to see Michael Rossi.

"I've decided to take your generous job offer," Joseph said without feeling or emotion. "I'll do whatever you want me to in your organization. Just don't ever ask me to kill somebody. That's something I could never do."

"Don't worry; I have enough men in my organization to take care of that aspect. Besides, I want you to learn the business ins and outs so you'll be able to take over, run the whole ball of wax. When I'm gone, you'll be the top dog."

"Just show me what to do," Joseph said. Inside he felt empty. He had fought the devil and the devil won. He conceded the battle. The only thing that kept him going in life had been his love for Jennie. And now even that was gone, over, finished.

He kept busy, so busy he wouldn't think. And he stayed away from the Casino so he wouldn't run into them again. He learned about the matrix of the organization, where the money went, where it was kept, who owed what, and their commodities: mostly drugs and prostitution. Joseph had pangs of guilt whenever he thought about the Lord but he quickly pushed it away. God had let him down, why should he feel guilty about anything.

And in spite of himself, in quiet moments, he relived his lips claiming hers, their moments of passion. Then he would drive himself harder, anything to forget.

Michael Rossi was proud to have his son by his side after all the lost and wasted years. And he wanted everyone to know that Joseph was to take over the organization. He planned a large dinner party with everyone on his staff there as well as the heads of the other families. He planned to drop the bombshell at the dinner. The other families would be understandably upset. Some of them had their eyes on his organization and would love to see him die, or be killed, so they could grab a lion's share of the business.

Jennie was getting dressed. She didn't know Joseph would be there because she didn't know that Gary worked for Michael Rossi. All she knew is that he worked for a mob boss as a runner.

Her mind was on Joseph as usual and when Gary grabbed her and kissed her, she moaned, "Oh Joseph."

Gary suddenly pulled back and punched her in the face. His ring cut her below her eye and it quickly took on a bluish tint. "Don't ever call me that again! That's one thing I won't tolerate from you. I'm not Joseph and don't ever make that mistake again. Now fix your face and try to cover the bruise up. I hate to have to lie and make up excuses for you."

Gary had no way of knowing that Joseph would be at the dinner. It was for his boss and all of the men involved in the mob. He didn't know about Joseph's relationship to Michael Rossi and he felt good about his position there. He was sure he would work his way up the ladder and become Mr. Rossi's right hand man in time.

Although he did wonder about Joseph turning up in the same state, the same city, the same Casino where they were. This puzzled him and he couldn't figure it out. This was too much for a coincidence. It had even crossed his mind that Joseph tracked them there, but he didn't think that was possible. "All very confusing." He thought.

Gary and Jennie entered the ballroom where the dinner was being held. She wore a gown of gold lamé and she looked stunning in it with her dark hair. The gown had little spaghetti straps with a low cut bodice and the skirt hugged the curves of her figure. She wore her hair up and had a small tiara over her forehead, with wisps of hair falling down over it where it just peeped out from her hair. All of the men looked in her direction when she entered.

There were long tables set up with nametags by each place, and Gary and Jennie were seated on the left of Michael Rossi, with him at the head of the table. Joseph was on the right. All three of them looked surprised to see the other.

Joseph quickly turned his eyes in a different direction but Jennie noticed a hard set to his jaw, a steely resolve in his face and it broke her heart because she knew that it was because of her that it was there.

Gary was not too pleased either. He wondered what on earth Joseph was doing there, especially seated next to the big man himself. He pinched Jennie to make sure she understood her place.

All of the men had beautiful women by their sides, dressed to kill. Joseph and Michael were the only two who didn't have dates. But to Michael, this was business, not pleasure. Although it would bring pleasure to him to introduce his long lost son.

Joseph didn't miss the way she looked and it stirred the hate up more to know that she was so beautiful, that every man in the room would look at her and desire her. He had taken note of the tiara and the way she was wearing her hair. It was just as she wore it on their wedding day and this too brought a raging hate for her.

And even while he felt the hatred stirred up, he wished with all of his heart that he could trade places with Gary. "She's sure changed," he thought. "She's become a woman, all woman." And he desired her more than ever before.

Jennie secretly watched Joseph from under her long lashes without anyone being the wiser. She remembered what he had told her about

Michael Rossi and the bitterness in his voice as he spoke about him. And she wondered if she had anything to do with him being here with the famous Mafia leader.

In spite of the make up on her face, Joseph noticed the cut under her eye and the bruise beginning to take shape. But he wouldn't let himself dwell on anything that concerned her. She was dead to him and that's how he would keep it.

Michael Rossi waited until his guests were well into the meal before he stood up and tapped his fork on the water glass. "My friends," he said while waving his arms to include them all, "tonight is a very special night for me. A night I've waited all my life for. I know a lot of you have wondered what would happen to the organization if something should happen to me. Well tonight I'm proud to say that the whole business, the whole organization, will be taken over by my son Joseph." He beamed in Joseph's direction while pulling his arm to get him to rise.

Joseph rose stiffly, trying hard to put a smile on his face as he faced them. He heard gasps all over the room but he thought he heard a soft, "no Joseph!" come from Jennie's direction. He didn't look at her. He just bowed slightly in acknowledgement of their claps and congratulations, welcoming him into the family.

Gary almost choked on the food he was eating. He couldn't believe his bad luck. Of all people to get ahead of him in the chain of command! It seemed like Joseph was forever in front of him, claiming what he himself should by rights, have.

Jennie lowered her eyes. She didn't want to look at Joseph. She felt a guilt so deep she didn't think she could ever get over it. She knew why he did this: to spite her, to get even with her for hurting him, for embracing the enemy.

The rest of the night was a blur. She hardly knew what she said or did. Joseph wouldn't even look in her direction. "He must really hate me," she thought. "There's no way I can ever win him back now."

Chavez secretly watched Joseph. He saw the hard, steely resolve around him and knew that something had happened to change him. Chavez himself loved Joseph as he had loved his father before him. He took it upon himself to be Joseph's bodyguard and Michael never objected. He almost thought it was fitting, since Chavez had followed him around when he was Joseph's age.

Chavez set it in his mind to find out what troubled Joseph. He had changed since he came to Las Vegas. So he watched and listened. It wasn't long before he noticed the change that took place in his manner whenever Jennie's name was mentioned.

And she was mentioned often by the men in Michael Rossi's employ. They all admired her beauty and thought that it was wasted on Gary. So they talked about her and each secretly had a desire to have her for their own.

Chavez decided to help Joseph. If this woman was the one Joseph was upset over, then Chavez would help him all he could.

Chavez entered Joseph's office in the Penthouse where Joseph was going over the figures, practically engulfed in papers spread out around him. This organization's reach was wide and it boggled his mind to know all that took place daily.

"Hey Joseph, Gary must have lost his key. I'm sure his suite is 354 and I found this downstairs. Gary is out collecting tonight so I'll just leave it on the table for him to get tomorrow." Chavez said offhandedly.

Joseph nodded as he watched Chavez leave the room. His heart was pounding and his hands were sweaty. He could no more control his actions than he could control his heartbeat. He walked to the table and put the key in his pocket.

"I have to go out tonight Jennie, and I'm just not sure that I trust you," Gary said. "I'd better make sure you stay put."

He came toward her with a syringe and she cried, "No Gary, please, not that again. I promise I won't leave the room."

"There, there, sweets. This is just a precaution to make sure you're a good girl for me." He injected the drug in her arm and she felt herself slipping, that familiar darkness overtaking her.

Later that night as Jennie lay on the chaise lounge in the darkened room, she vaguely heard the door open and thought Gary had come back. She was still under the effects of the drug, but had more moments that were lucid due to her tolerance from so many shots. With the room so dark, all she saw was an outline of a man who she thought was Gary coming toward her. He sat beside her and took her in his arms. She stiffened up until he started kissing her. Then she knew it wasn't Gary, it was Joseph. And she kissed him with wild abandon. "Oh how I've missed this," she thought. His hands were on her in familiar ways and she thought she would die with the sheer joy of the moment.

"Joseph, Joseph," she cried. "I've missed you so much."

"Yeah," he said bitterly, "so much that you dropped everything to become his mistress." He could tell that she'd been drugged. He knew so well from the past all about it.

"Oh Joseph," she cried, "you must leave before he comes back, he'll kill the baby."

He thought it was the drugs talking. "Hush love." He continued kissing her like a hungry man, even while he hated himself for being there. She was like a drug to him. He couldn't do without her. Even while his flesh hated his need, he desired her.

"Jennie, Jennie, let's leave here, go away together. It'll be like it was before."

"No, no! You don't understand! He'll kill you and the baby. He said he'd never let me go. He'll kill us all."

He heard someone fumbling with the key at the door so he quickly slipped out on the balcony. Gary came in and saw her hair all tousled, her lips red from passionate kisses. He grabbed her by the hair and slapped her face over and over.

Joseph had already climbed up to the other floor. If he had stayed, he would have killed Gary on the spot.

Joseph avoided her like the plague. His own body had betrayed him and he didn't want it to happen again. He vowed to keep the hate alive, even while he fantasized about her being in his arms.

And while he vowed to stay away from her, he was busy giving Gary a larger territory, more travel time involved.

Chavez walked around with a silly grin on his face. He had noticed the missing key, which returned a few hours later. He knew he had been right. And he was glad he could help Joseph. He would easily and quickly murder Gary and dispose of the body if Joseph asked him to.

Chavez was a large man, tall and muscular with only a hint of a gut forming in the middle. He had been with Michael for many years and was as faithful as an old hound. But his loyalties were quickly being transferred to Joseph. There was a goodness about Joseph that he hadn't sensed in Michael; something different and unique. And Chavez liked what he saw. Somehow, he didn't understand it, but somehow he felt as if he had a destiny with Joseph.

He had no loyalty at all to Gary, just barely tolerated his presence, and only because he had no choice. In fact, Gary was not well liked by anyone in the Las Vegas mob. But they were all loyal to Michael and respected Michael's choice of runners. And they all admired Jennie.

The men all hung around the Penthouse during the day and that's all they seemed to talk about was Jennie's beauty, how it was wasted on Gary. None of the men liked Gary and they all begrudged the fact that he had such a beautiful woman with him. There was one man, Bradley Johnson, who watched Jennie and secretly wished that Gary would disappear from the face of the earth.

Jennie herself didn't know that anyone watched her or even cared what happened to her. She was so tired of the beatings, the humiliations that Gary put her through just to prove his ownership of her. She cried often when he wasn't around and wished she could get away from him, go anyplace just to get away, even if for a short time. "But," she thought, "where could I go and what good would it do? I can't take any chances with Joshua's life."

She was constantly reminded by Gary that she would be killing her child if she didn't do as he said. Moreover, she knew that he meant it. Gary wasn't one to issue idle threats. So she stayed, and wished that she were dead.

And Gary continued to do any and everything that he could to her to make her miserable. Even though he loved her, he knew deep down in his heart that she would never really be his, and that ate at him, festered like a skin cancer.

"If only there was something I could do to take Joseph completely out of her mind," he thought. "Maybe I could hit her over the head and give her amnesia again. She certainly forgot about Joseph in the past. But with my luck she'd forget about me. I'll just have to keep beating and humiliating her to keep her in line. She might think she loves

Joseph, but she'll never get the chance to be in his arms again. I'll chain her to the bed if I have to."

When he thought about Jennie chained to the bed, it produced a picture in his mind that he enjoyed and he continued to think about it. "Maybe that's what I'll have to do," he thought.

Chapter Thirteen

Joseph stood on the balcony overlooking the pool, deep in thought. He had to break all ties with Jennie. He had to get her out of his system and he was determined to do so. He kept feeding into the hate, telling himself that she ran to Gary the first chance she got. He even considered turning him in to the DA in Louisiana, but then he remembered that he too was on the lam, wanted for murder.

He was watching a couple by the pool. She was lying with her face down and the guy was putting lotion on her back. Then it dawned on him that it was Jennie and Gary. He watched as she sat up and went to leave, but Gary pulled her by the hair and she fell back on the chaise lounge. Joseph seethed with rage but then he reminded himself, that's what she wants. Maybe she likes it. Maybe that was the problem; he was too gentle with her. He'd show her. Two could play that same game. He would find himself a date and flaunt her just as Jennie flaunted Gary.

He privately talked to some of the guys who hung around all the time in the Penthouse. Joseph and Michael each had an office here where they took care of the Organization's business. The guys who hung around were the "security" guys, Michael's personal bodyguards.

Joseph wanted to meet somebody and T Ball had a girlfriend who had a friend. She was a showgirl, tall and willowy, blonde hair and blue eyes. The total opposite of Jennie and for that he was glad.

He met her down in the Casino and they had dinner in the Casino restaurant, and then browsed the gaming tables. He kept hoping he would run into them, and finally he spotted them at the Blackjack table. He brought his date Coral closer to where they sat, waiting for them to notice him. Finally, Jennie saw him and by that time, Coral was hanging all over him.

Jennie flushed and turned away. She couldn't help thinking how good he looked. He was wearing a white sports coat & white pants, with a black shirt open at the neck.

At the moment she hated Coral and wished she was the one hanging on to him. She tried not to look but found that she couldn't keep her eyes away from their direction. Gary didn't notice them, he was so absorbed in the blackjack game before him.

She never drank but tonight when the waitress passed by, she took a drink from the tray that she carried. She took a swallow and almost choked it was so nasty. But after a few swallows it went down smoothly. Gary noticed her with a drink and wondered what was going on with her. He knew she never drank, didn't even believe in it because of her mother.

Finally, Gary saw Joseph and Coral and surmised the reason for the drink. It did him good to see Joseph with someone else for a change. Maybe he would leave them alone now.

Joseph casually walked in their direction with Coral on his arm and pretended to see them at the gaming table. "Well hello Gary, Jennie. Having any luck?"

"A little," Gary answered. "I see you had some luck tonight already."

"Oh forgive me, this is Coral. Coral honey, this is Gary and Jennie."

Jennie grabbed another drink from the waitresses' tray and gulped it down. Joseph looked at her with one eyebrow raised. He had never known her to take a drink. So his plan must be working. "Let her eat her heart out," he thought.

Aloud Joseph said, "Would you two want to join us in the lounge for a drink? Looks like Jennie's had a head start on us."

"Sure," Gary said. "How about it sweets, want to go have a drink?"

Jennie shrugged her shoulders.

Joseph noticed that she had new bruises on her arm, as if someone had grabbed her very hard. His gut tightened up just at the picture of

Gary hurting her. He told himself that it was because he didn't like to see anyone hurt. He still hated her with everything in him.

They settled in a booth in the lounge and ordered a drink. Jennie didn't know what she had been drinking so she didn't know what to order. Gary ordered for her. "Bring her an old fashioned," he told the waitress.

As they chatted and made small talk, Joseph noticed that she was quiet, not talking at all. That wasn't like Jennie. She used to be so self assured, so outgoing. He felt a sadness watching this new woman, so unlike the Jennie he had come to know and love.

Jennie herself was feeling woozy from the drink, and angry for the way Coral was hanging on to her husband. But it wasn't her place to say anything; after all she was here with Gary. And she was ever mindful of Joshua. She didn't have the right to do anything to make Gary mad. She had to think about Joshua.

Gary was a born flirt, and he didn't make an exception with Coral. He flirted openly with her and finally asked her to dance with him. Jennie was thankful when they left.

Joseph was quiet for a while, and then he spoke. "I've never seen you drink Jennie. I thought you didn't want to because of your mother."

"Maybe I didn't know what I was missing," she replied flippantly.

"Better be careful. Tomorrow you'll find out exactly what you've missed."

"Well tomorrow's another day and I'll worry about it when it comes," she answered.

"Come on, let's dance. At least if you think Gary won't mind." He said.

She didn't answer that last remark, just stood up to dance. And once she was in his arms, everyone else ceased to exist. "What is it about him?" she wondered for the umpteenth time. "Just his touch and I fall under his spell."

He held her tight and she pressed closer into him. "Jennie," he whispered.

She loved it when he whispered her name. It was an intimate thing, something just between them.

He kept telling himself that he hated her with every fiber of his being, but holding her like this, her warmth next to his body, her scent in his nostrils, he thought he would die from the sheer joy of being this close to her.

He remembered her sitting on his lap, nuzzling his neck, of dancing with her at other times, of being weak with her very nearness.

And Jennie was in heaven, just clinging to Joseph, this man she loved with a passionate love, an all-consuming love. How could their love be denied? When he whispered her name, she went weak all over. When he kissed her hair, she wanted to seek his lips, get lost in the passion that was always there, always between them. She had forgotten that Gary existed, that Coral existed. There was just the two of them, and there was this love, this passion that couldn't be denied.

Although Gary was totally absorbed with Coral, he didn't miss the way they held on to one another. He guessed he would have to teach her a lesson when they got home. And that thought excited him. He found that more and more he was enjoying it when he had to hurt her.

He knew Jennie was getting drunk and he resolved to take her home soon before she made a fool of herself. He had never seen her take a drink and it made him seethe with rage knowing why she was drinking.

No matter what he did, he couldn't seem to take Joseph out of her mind, out of her heart and it caused a rage in him just to think about it. "She'll get hers tonight," he thought, and that thought gave him a little satisfaction.

Chapter Fourteen

Joseph knew that Gary had accounts to pick up today and would be gone most of the day. He fingered the key in his pocket. Chavez had left it on the table and since Gary never mentioned it, Joseph had just kept it. He thought he would be strong and not use it again. But he found himself in front of her door, unlocking it and going in.

Jennie was sprawled out on the bed face down, and when he tried to turn her over she moaned, "Please, don't move me. Oh God, I'm so sick."

He got a wet washcloth and started bathing her face. "I told you you'd be sorry. This is your first hangover and I'll bet you never forget it."

"Ow," she cried when he wiped her cheek, and he noticed the bruise. Gary must have been mad because they danced last night.

"Did Gary beat you up Jennie?"

She just shrugged her shoulders. "I can't remember anything."

He picked up the phone and called Chavez. "Chavez, bring a bloody Mary down here to room 354." To Jennie he said, "You need a little hair of the dog."

Chavez brought the drink and Joseph insisted that Jennie drink it. She didn't want to but he kept saying it would make her feel better. She drank it to shut him up, and was surprised to find that it did help her some.

"Jennie I need to talk to you about something. Are you alert? He didn't drug you this time did he?"

"No."

"Well back in Louisiana I've been charged with your murder."

"What?" She asked, shocked.

"Yeah, they think I murdered you and I had a trial and all. Well, they found me guilty. That's when Michael Rossi paid to help me escape from prison."

"Oh Joseph, it must have been horrible."

"To say the least. But I need you to get in touch with the DA and tell him you're alive. I need to get the charges dropped."

"Of course, I'll do it as soon as I can. I...."

Her words were cut off when she heard someone at the door. Joseph quickly left by the balcony and she lay down again.

"Hello love," Gary said. "I see you're alone this time. I guess my methods of persuasion worked. How are you feeling?" Then he noticed the empty glass on the bedside table. "Where'd you get this? Has he been here already this morning?"

"No Gary, I called room service and got something to settle my stomach. I didn't feel too good when I woke up."

"Yeah, I'll just bet." He grabbed her and shook her. "What does it take to get him out of your mind? Do I have to squeeze the life out of you?" He put his hands on her throat and squeezed until she felt herself blacking out.

When she came to Gary was gone. She felt like she didn't want to live anymore. What was the use? She couldn't have Joseph or their son. Why keep going on? She wanted to die but wasn't sure she could commit suicide. She didn't know if she was strong enough for that.

The door opened and when she looked up, she saw Joseph; but even his presence didn't cheer her up. It was too late for them, too late for anything in life that brought her happiness.

"Jennie, are you ok? I was worried about you." He sat on the bed beside her and noticed the redness on her neck. He touched it tenderly. "Did he do this to you Jennie?" Before she could even answer, he cried out with emotion, "Why do you stay with him? What hold does he have over you?"

She couldn't answer. She could never tell him about Joshua. Or Gary would surely have him killed. And she could never be the one to sign his death warrant.

"I can't see you anymore Joseph. Please don't come here again. It's just causing trouble, more trouble than I can bear."

The flatness of her tone tugged at his heart. He had heard that same dead pan tone when she had given up on life once before.

"If that's what you want Jennie, then I'll stay away. I didn't realize that you loved Gary so much that you would take anything he handed you." His voice was turning bitter, "I hope you and he will be very happy together. And here's a parting gift to remember me by."

He pulled her to himself roughly. He kissed her savagely, like he'd never kissed her before, wanting to hurt her, to cause her to feel pain like he felt. Soon he was lost in the nearness of her, he couldn't help it. No matter how hard he tried to hate her, to hurt her, he always caved in the end. And she always responded, always kissed him with all the passion she felt for him.

He pulled away and pushed her aside, trying to humiliate her. He just didn't understand the depth of her uncaring soul at that moment. She was past hurting.

Gary came home later that day and made her get dressed. "I've got more business to take care of and I'm not leaving you alone any more. From now on, where I go, you go."

She didn't protest, just did as she was told. What did it matter where he took her? One place was as good as the other.

How wrong she was. He did business in some of the low class dives in Las Vegas, places Jennie would never have willingly gone if she had had a choice. He left her at the bar to fend for herself while he concluded his business in back rooms.

The men in the bar would sidle up to her; some even so bold as to grab her and try to kiss her. One greasy fellow tried this and she thought again about suicide. Anything was better than this humiliation. She fought him off as he tried to pull her to himself, but the bartender had pity on her and made him leave her alone.

In every bar, it was the same. The same lowly creatures who saw her beauty and wanted her. And because she was there and seemingly alone, they all got ideas. In one place, there were several truckers playing pool and one of them grabbed her. When she fought and tried to get away, he just laughed. His friends got in on the game and they just kept grabbing her while they circled around her.

Something in her snapped and she started screaming and she couldn't stop. Gary came running out but the men acted as if she was screaming for no reason, as if she had just flipped her lid. He started slapping her to get her to be quiet but she couldn't stop screaming. Finally, he punched her out and carried her to the car.

The stories got back to Joseph of course. The bodyguards sat around all day and had nothing to do but talk. So they would talk about her, about how Gary didn't deserve her, how he was dragging her around town with him to the low class places.

One man related what had happened when Gary had to punch her out. "I heard that Jennie started screaming and she couldn't stop. Gary started slapping her face over and over but she couldn't stop screaming. So he punched her and when she went out, he threw her over his shoulder and carried her to the car."

Joseph couldn't understand why Jennie put up with all that Gary did to her. This just wasn't like the Jennie he'd known in the past. "Oh God, what has happened to my Jennie? Please God, help her."

Joseph knew that there had to be a reason and since he couldn't see any, he assumed that she was so in love with Gary that she would put up with whatever he did to her. And this broke his heart. And even as he vowed to make her love him again, a spirit of dejection settled on him, because he knew it was hopeless. If she loved Gary so much that she would put up with beatings, humiliations, and God only knew what else, then there was no hope for him.

The best thing that Joseph could do would be to get over her. Just put her from his mind and pretend she didn't exist. But even as he thought about that, he knew in his heart that it was impossible. There would always be Jennie in his life in one way or another. Even if she disappeared and he never saw her again, he knew that he would continue to love her until the day he died.

Some of the guys thought it was funny what Gary did to her, but others felt pity for her. Joseph thought seriously about having Chavez 'rub him out' as the guys were so fond of saying when they spoke of getting rid of someone.

Chavez himself watched Joseph and noticed the way he looked when he heard those things about Jennie and once offered to get rid of Gary. "You want me to make him disappear, boss?"

"No, but thanks anyway Chavez." He added, "I'll let you know if I change my mind though."

Chapter Fifteen

Joseph decided to exercise some of his authority as the next in line mob boss. He instructed T Ball to send a man, one who was unknown in the mob, to follow Gary from place to place as he took up his collections. This man was to be one that T Ball trusted to be discreet; and one that could fade in the background without causing too much attention to himself. He was to be a bodyguard to Jennie without Gary realizing it.

From then on, Jennie didn't have any more trouble from unwanted advances as she sat and waited for Gary to make his collections.

Poncho was a huge Mexican man who always showed up and sat two stools down from her. If anyone got any ideas, his presence soon discouraged them. Jennie herself might have figured it out, but she was thankful that she didn't have to endure what she had in the past.

Joseph kept his word and stayed away from her. It took a superhuman effort on his part but he continued to attempt to stay busy as well as feed the hate to keep it alive. He kept reminding himself that this is what she chose. She could leave Gary any time she wanted to but she obviously loved him and was willing to put up with anything he did to her.

And in a way he could relate to that. For he was willing to put up with what she was doing to him and in spite of trying to maintain a hate for her, in his weaker moments he knew that he loved her and would die for her if called upon to do it. She would always be his Jennie, his love.

He didn't know how, but she must have gotten in touch with the DA back in New Orleans because when he called Lois Miller, she told him that he had been cleared of all charges. He arranged with Social

Services for Lois to get his son and keep him at the Plantation until he could get back there and get him. He just didn't feel like it was appropriate to bring him here to Las Vegas, and he had no way to keep him here. He knew Lois would take good care of Joshua.

It crossed his mind that now he could go back to Louisiana, that there was no reason to stay in Las Vegas. But even as he thought that, Jennie's face came into his thoughts and he knew that nothing on earth could entice him to leave here as long as she was here.

Michael Rossi called Joseph into his office. It was seldom that he did this and Joseph was curious as to what he could want.

"Joseph, I just want to warn you to be careful. One of the other family heads, Joe Ditz, has his eye on our organization. I heard rumors that he plans to start a mob war. He may even come after you and me. That would help clear the way for a take over. You probably need to call a meeting of everyone in the mob and warn them to be on their toes."

Joseph nodded. "I'll take care of it." He wondered if Gary would bring her to the meeting.

He sent word around to all the men that they were going to have a meeting in the downstairs ballroom at noon. He notified the kitchen to have tables set up for lunch. It felt good to be able to command and have people jump to obey. He could see how power and authority could go to one's head.

Michael sat next to Joseph but he motioned for Joseph to take over. He was glad to see that Gary had indeed brought Jennie, and he secretly watched her when he could. He felt like he could instill his strength into her just by willing it on her as he watched her. And he longed to be alone with her, just to hold her in his arms.

The mantle of leadership sat well on Joseph's shoulders, as if he was born to it. Being a cop had put enough self-assurance into him to carry him now, and Michael was so proud of him he thought he'd burst.

Jennie was proud of him too. She didn't like the role he walked in, but he carried it well. She had missed him so much that her eyes hungrily drank in the sight of him. And Gary sat there and sulked.

"We're under a war watch, men. There's a rumor that Joe Ditz might try to start a mob war to get to us. You all need to be on guard and expect anything to come at you. He'll probably try to hit me or Michael, so be on your toes."

When he said that last, Jennie looked at him with real fear in her eyes. A look that he didn't miss. And it warmed his heart that she was afraid for him. He'd take any crumbs he could get. He glanced at Gary and saw that he was drinking heavily, arm bent at the elbow continuously.

Joseph assigned certain men to stay with Michael at all times, and certain ones to stay around him. He didn't want to take any chances. If he were killed, Gary would end up the winner and he couldn't bear to think about that. He would not only have his wife, but he would get his child also.

The thought flickered across his mind that Jennie didn't ask about their child, but then he thought, "Maybe she figures I don't know where he's at since I wasn't around when he was born. What a mixed up situation." He also thought briefly about what she had said, that Gary would kill him and Joshua, even her. He attributed it to the drugs, but just a glimmer of something was there. He just didn't know what.

As lunch progressed, Gary continued to drink more than he ate. He was eaten up with jealousy over Joseph being put in charge of the mob. He knew that he himself would make a better leader. Joseph just didn't have that killer instinct that it took. But he knew that he had it. Hadn't he proved it when it was necessary?

The more he drank, the more sullen he got and Jennie was worried. She knew that at times like this he would find a reason to take his frustration out on her. An unfamiliar thought popped into her mind, "Oh God, please let him just pass out." She hadn't prayed in so long it didn't even seem to be coming from her. She still lacked some of her memories from the past, and prayer was one of them.

Joseph was worried too. He knew that Gary was in a sullen mood and he feared for Jennie's welfare. He whispered something to Chavez and Chavez nodded before leaving the room. He returned a while later and made the man next to Gary move so he could talk to Gary. As he spoke to him, he called the waiter over and gave Gary the drink that had been prepared ahead of time. Joseph watched him down the drink in a few gulps and was satisfied.

Gary passed out at the table and Joseph had some of the men carry him to his room. He knew that he'd be out for hours. Chavez took

Jennie by the arm and led her from the room, but put her instead in Joseph's suite.

Joseph dismissed the meeting and hurried upstairs. He felt like a nervous beau going to meet his first girl. He wasn't sure how Jennie would take this.

"Hi Jennie," he said when he entered. She was standing by the patio and the sunlight shone on her in a way that reminded him that she was God's anointed. Something they both seemed to have forgotten.

"Joseph... Why are you doing this? I asked you to leave me alone."

He had crossed the room and was face to face with her. "I need to hear it again," he said as he took her in his arms. "I need you to say you don't love me, that you don't want to be around me. That you love Gary."

He pulled her to him and she didn't resist. She couldn't utter the words he had spoken. She was lost in his kisses and wondered again why she was cursed to fall into his arms every time he touched her. Just his nearness sent her over the edge. She forgot everyone else in the world but her Joseph. She got weak as he smothered her with kisses. He kissed every inch of her face, and then trailed kisses down her neck. She even forgot about Joshua for a time. This ecstasy was all she craved, all she wanted in this world. He was her beloved and she lost herself in him.

And Joseph swore to himself that he would win her back. He would make her love him again. He knew that he couldn't live without her and thought about long, lonely years in the future with no Jennie. He wouldn't want to live if she weren't in his future. From the first time he had seen her, he had been lost. There was just something about her, something that drew him like a magnet. Or maybe it was because God had put them together, and nothing could separate them. No matter what she did, no matter where she went or who she was with, yet he loved her with an all-consuming love that even time couldn't erase. That the forces of darkness couldn't hold back.

"Jennie, Jennie," he groaned. "Why can't I live without you? Why am I lost every time I pull you into my arms? Tell me that you love me," he demanded. "Say it!"

"I love you, I love you, oh Joseph I love you so much." She said. She couldn't help it. She never wanted to let him go. This is where she belonged. This is where she was safe from Gary, safe from everything that threatened her world.

"Then stay with me love," he murmured. "We'll go away together."

She was jolted back to her senses with those words. She could never stay here where she was safe. She had to remember Joshua. She couldn't sign his death warrant. She pulled away from him and ran from the room.

Chapter Sixteen

Gary was not at all happy when he woke up. He knew that he had been drugged—and assumed that Jennie and Joseph had planned it so they could be together. The more he thought about it, the madder he got, until he was consumed with rage.

He pulled a sleeping Jennie from the bed and started hitting her as he'd never hit her before. He was literally trying to beat her to death and she knew it. She started screaming and he kept dragging her toward the balcony. She knew that it was his intention to throw her off.

"Boss, come quick," Chavez said. "I think Gary's killin' her."

Joseph grabbed his gun and they ran downstairs. They could hear her screaming from the hall. Joseph opened the door with the key he had and saw Gary trying to throw her off the balcony. He went crazy at the sight and fired at Gary. Gary fell to the floor, blood flowing from the bullet wound in his back. A puddle of bright red blood began to pool under him.

"No..." Jennie screamed. She dropped to the floor over the dead body and started shaking him. "You can't die, please Gary don't die." All the while, she was crying and screaming at him, "What have you done Joseph? Oh God, please don't let him die!"

Joseph turned around and walked out of her life.

There had been three attempts on Joseph's life in the last few weeks. He wondered if his guardian angels still hung around. At this point, he really didn't care. God had even deserted him. He had lost everything he ever loved and made up his mind that he didn't need any of them. He'd just get through life the best he could, doing what he had to, to stay alive. Or maybe he'd get lucky and one of the hit men would get him. Then it would be all over with; this cold empty feeling inside that was killing him. He didn't have to convince himself to hate her anymore. It was there for real.

Chavez took care of the body and got someone to clean up the blood in the room. Jennie just sat and stared in the distance. Chavez didn't know the story behind her and Joseph, but a great compassion for Jennie filled him. He just didn't believe that she hurt Joseph the way she had been doing all this while, without a good reason.

That special feeling he had for Joseph, now extended to Jennie. He came in daily to bring her food and gently tried to coax her into eating it. He hired a woman to come in, groom her, and make sure she was taken care of. He didn't tell Joseph any of this because he didn't think Joseph would like it. He had seen something die in Joseph that day and it broke his heart for the two of them. He never mentioned any of it to Michael or any of the other men. This was his secret.

Jennie was numb inside. She wanted to cry but the pain was too deep; far too deep for mere tears. It lay there as a lump, and she couldn't cry. She went through the motions each day, not even realizing what she was doing. A kindly woman was there taking care of her, helping her bathe and dress, sitting her down and gently chiding her for not eating. She lost weight. She prayed for death. Anything to erase the image of her little baby being murdered. The image consumed her. She dreamed about it all night, and thought about it all day. She wished she had some of Gary's drugs now. She wished the blackness would overtake her so she didn't have to think.

She didn't know where Joseph was and didn't care. He had signed their child's death warrant. Something she had suffered so long to avoid. She didn't miss Gary, was in fact glad that she didn't have to put up with all he did to her; then she would feel guilty. "I'd gladly have put up with more if I could have saved my baby," she thought.

The two angels watched with interest all that went on in Joseph and Jennie's life. They knew that it was all in the Father's plan and they didn't question what the Father set in motion. But they watched them, and they watched the demons hanging around, gleefully shouting curses at them. It had worked out so well from the demons standpoint. They just kept hanging around and rejoicing that they had won the victory!

Chavez continued to visit Jennie. Sometimes he would just sit in the room with her, not saying anything. Sometimes he would try to get her to go out and get some fresh air. She always ignored him. She was lost in a world that he didn't understand: a world that contained nothing but her guilt.

He brought little bouquets of flowers to her and when she ignored him, he just put them in water and set them on the table by her. He thought that if he could brighten up her surroundings, that awful look of pain would leave her face.

He was a kind man and Jennie would have appreciated all he did if the situation had been different. She even wondered briefly why he did it. She didn't think Joseph had put him up to it. She didn't think she would ever see or hear from Joseph again. And she was almost glad. That would be her penance, maybe it would help ease the guilt. She should have convinced Gary to take her away from Joseph sooner. Then this wouldn't have happened. It was all her fault. She was the one who should have made sure that nothing like this could have happened.

Joseph was reckless, as if he sought out death at every turn. T Ball knew that he had killed Gary, and figured that Gary had it coming. But he didn't know the depth of emotion in Joseph's heart, the depth of hate he felt for Jennie. He just couldn't understand why Joseph was being so careless. Almost as if he welcomed death.

Joseph surrounded himself with beautiful showgirls. Everywhere he went, he had two or three with him. He was trying to soothe his crippled ego. He drank more than he should have, trying to reach a place of numbness so he wouldn't feel the pain as bad.

Jennie stayed lost in her own world. And Chavez never gave up on her. He visited her daily until she started to acknowledge his presence. He finally talked her into going downstairs with him to supper. She was far too thin, almost getting to the point where she looked sickly.

They entered the restaurant and sat in a booth near the back. She even made small talk with Chavez. She was starting to feel a fondness for him; he was becoming a father figure to her. His many little kindnesses really touched her heart. She was a stranger to him, and yet he seemed to care whether she lived or died. More than she herself cared.

Joseph entered the restaurant with a showgirl on each arm. When he saw them, he stopped dead in his tracks, and then proceeded to sit at a booth on the side away from them. "What's she doing here with Chavez?" He wondered. "What's he got up his sleeve? She looks so bad, she must really be grieving." He thought bitterly. He wouldn't acknowledge that he even saw them. He laughed louder and drank more than he had recently.

Jennie saw them of course. She couldn't help it. And she heard his loud laughter, and knew that he was trying to prove to her that he didn't need her. He was having fun with his new girls. She wanted to cry but then she reminded herself that this was, after all, her penance.

Chavez didn't miss a thing—the look on Joseph's face—and the look on hers. He got bold with Jennie, something he normally didn't do. He didn't like to interfere in someone else's life.

"What's goin' on Miss Jennie? I know you couldn't have loved Gary so much that you're grieving for him. There's more going on here than we see on the surface."

She started crying softly, her emerald eyes filling up with tears and creeping down her cheeks. She felt the need to talk to someone. She had kept everything bottled up so long, she felt as if she would explode if she didn't tell him. After all, he seemed like a father to her now.

"I hated Gary with a passion," she said heatedly. "I'd never grieve over him. But by his death, Joseph and I caused the death of our son."

"I don't understand," he said, surprised at this revelation. "I didn't know you two had a son."

"We were married only a few months when I conceived a son. When I was kidnapped in New Orleans they induced labor. I was kept drugged most of the time so everything is a big blur now, but they were going to sacrifice my son to the devil. It was a satanic cult, you see. Gary kept me drugged and brought me out here. He said that he had rescued my son from the cult and was keeping him with some friends, and if they didn't hear from him every now and then, they had orders to kill Joshua. He also said if I told Joseph or anyone, then I would be signing his death warrant. I couldn't tell Joseph. And now Gary's dead." She put her face in her hands and sobbed quietly.

Chavez suddenly remembered the night Michael Rossi gave the baby to Joseph. Now it all made sense. He had forgotten about that, didn't realize that Jennie was the mother. And he remembered all that this young woman had gone through with Gary and he was filled with a deep compassion for her.

"I'm sorry Miss Jennie," he said softly. "But listen," he went on, "we've got some good men in the organization in New Orleans. I'll have them nose around and see if they can find out anything, maybe find someone who knew Gary."

"Thanks Chavez. You're a good person. But please...please don't tell Joseph. I've made him hate me so passionately; I don't want to add to it by letting him know that he's responsible for his son's death. I couldn't bear it."

"Ok," he nodded. "It'll just be between us right now. I'll have the guys start on it immediately. But you got to promise me you'll start taking care of yourself. If we should find these friends of Gary's before...well before it's too late, you'll need your strength."

She nodded.

"Blow your nose now and eat your supper." He told her. "You look like a ghost you're so pale."

She dutifully blew her nose and tried to eat but the food just seemed to stick in her throat when she swallowed. She really wanted to eat to please Chavez because right now, he was the only person who cared if she lived or died.

Her mind strayed to Joseph. She couldn't help it. His face would slip into her mind when she least expected it. She wondered if any of his showgirls would feel his embrace tonight and she felt a heavy spirit of depression settling on her.

Joseph wasn't the only one who welcomed death. She too welcomed it, anything to stop the thoughts of her little baby being murdered, probably being sacrificed to Satan. She remembered so long ago when Gary was in the satanic cult in New Orleans, and all the poor people who died because of it. Again, she was glad that he was dead. Then she would feel guilty all over again. And the guilt was eating her alive.

Chapter Seventeen

Joseph couldn't figure it out but his pride wouldn't let him ask questions. However, he paid more attention to the men when they started talking. He found out that Chavez had been bringing Jennie little bouquets of flowers almost daily.

Everyone was perplexed by this. Chavez was in his sixties and not prone to hanging around women. He had always seemed content to be Michael's bodyguard and now Joseph's as well.

They knew he was like a big lovable mutt so they assumed that he felt sorry for Jennie now that she was all alone. And she looked so pale and sickly. Maybe he was trying to nurse her back to health.

Their curiosity was piqued even further when he started taking her out to the pool daily so she could sit in the sun. They would eat lunch, and then she would lie in the sun until he brought her back upstairs. These two were the talk of the town among the men. That's all Joseph ever heard them talk about any more and he was getting tired of it.

He finally confronted Chavez. "Look Chavez, you're not doing your job. You're supposed to be my bodyguard, not someone else's baby sitter."

"Don't worry boss, I watch your back. I'm here if you need me. I served your father faithfully for over twenty-five years. I never took a day off. I guess taking a few hours a day off won't hurt anything will it?"

What could Joseph say? He had him there. So he never mentioned it again.

Jennie started to glow with the golden tan she was getting. The sun had put light streaks in her hair and she looked radiant. Her body was filling out again, thanks to Chavez's urging her to eat, and she was beginning to have hope again.

Chavez had located through the men in New Orleans, a few leads on Gary's life down there and the men were following up on it. He had even hired a private detective.

Gary had lied at first to Jennie when he said he had the child. Actually, he was working on getting him. Some old friends from New Orleans knew about Joseph's trial and that his baby was to be placed in a foster home. So his friends applied to become foster parents and ended up with the child living with them. Joseph didn't know all of this because he hadn't bothered to call Lois Miller back.

After he spoke to Social Services, a social worker went to the home to get the child but they had moved lock, stock and barrel. They were nowhere to be found. When Lois attempted to gain custody, she found out that the baby wasn't in the foster home after all and that in fact, they couldn't find the foster parents. But she had no way of contacting Joseph. She would have to wait until he got in touch with her to tell him.

Joseph saw her beauty returning, the radiance about her, and he hated her even more. He continued on his path of destruction, drinking all night, reckless living. He seemed to seek his own demise.

Michael Rossi found love. After all the years since Deborah left, he dared to love again. She was a beautiful redhead, thirty years younger than he was, and he couldn't see beyond his own feelings for her. He probably would have shot anyone who suggested that she was a gold digger.

He moved her into his penthouse and bought her anything she wanted. He would have been very surprised to find out that the main thing she wanted was Joseph.

Whenever she was alone a few minutes with Joseph, she would come and lean against him, trying to entice him to kiss her. He would push her away but it made him all the more desirable to her.

Joseph remembered another Joseph in the Bible, how his boss's wife wanted him and even lied about him, and Joseph tried to stay away from her. "That kind of complications I don't need." He thought.

Whenever he saw Jennie around the pool or in the restaurant, men were starting to flock to her and that made him hate her even more. He never could figure that one out, why he should hate her more because of it, but just accepted it. She was looking more beautiful than she ever had, and he knew it wouldn't take much for her to find another man. And when he thought about it, he would seethe with rage.

And he couldn't figure out this relationship with Chavez. They would walk together around the hotel grounds, always talking about something. He wondered what was transpiring between the two. He didn't think it was a love affair or anything, but just couldn't figure it out and that made him mad too. In fact, he got mad at everything that had anything to do with her. And every now and then when he least expected it, he would remember the feel of her lips on his and get mad at himself.

Michael Rossi was like a big kid with this newfound love. She had consented to become his bride and they planned the biggest wedding Las Vegas had seen. All the important people would be there, at least all the ones who had mob involvement. And all the heads of the families would come. He rented a large hall and hired the best decorators and wedding planners. He beamed when he walked around with her on his arm. And all the while she secretly watched Joseph.

Chapter Eighteen

C laire Worth was an ex-showgirl who had made the rounds. She had worked in all the Casino shows in town. She was tall, almost as tall as Michael was, but she was shapely in all the right places.

She was originally from San Francisco, but migrated to Las Vegas two years ago. She fell in love with a blackjack dealer and married him shortly after she arrived in town. A baby, a girl she named Morgan, was born to the union. But Claire was not the motherly type. When the marriage ended, she walked away and let her ex-husband keep the baby, who was under a year old by the time the marriage dissolved.

And now she was marrying one of the top Mafia bosses in Las Vegas. She had married once for love, now she would marry for money and power. She could find love anywhere, but wealth was something that had always eluded her until now.

Michael sent an invitation to Jennie as a so-called widow of an ex mob runner. He let her stay in the suite he had provided for her and Gary because he took care of his own. He never did find out what happened to Gary, he just knew that he had been shot. And that was commonplace around the mob so he didn't question it. He even forgot that Jennie was the mother of his grandson, the wife of Joseph. Everything had happened in New Orleans and seemed like another lifetime.

Some of the bodyguards who hung around the penthouse were competing for Jennie. Joseph had to endure the conversations because they didn't know of his involvement with her. Nobody understood the boss these days, he always seemed mad at something.

Jennie herself was getting frustrated. There had been no results and she was no closer to finding out who had her son. But Chavez had figured out a way to stall. Michael Rossi had tapped Gary's phone because he didn't fully trust him. So Chavez found a guy who was an expert at splicing together tapes to make it say what he wanted it to say. They went through Gary's little black book and called every number then played a tape they had put together.

Gary's voice would come on with, "Hey, this is Gary. Things are good here. Hope they're ok there. I'll keep in touch."

They weren't sure if they had reached the right people or not, but it was worth a try. Chavez tried to help her keep a positive attitude and he checked often with the detective in New Orleans. There were some leads, but nothing solid.

Michael's new found love, Claire Worth, had met Jennie and thought it was sad that she was alone, so she would have nobody but Jennie as her Matron of Honor. Jennie was not up to it but Chavez convinced her that Michael was a little goo goo eyed right now about this wedding thing and it was probably best if Jennie just complied.

As the day dawned, Jennie dressed in an emerald green silk gown that was stunning. Claire had chosen the dress and sent it up to Jennie. It flowed down from the waist in straight lines, similar to the gown she had worn to the Endymion ball and suddenly, for a moment, her stomach felt queasy remembering the past horror she had endured; the horror that she felt as if she was still trapped in.

She didn't think any further than going to the wedding. If she had, she would have realized that Michael would have a best man, and he would walk with Jennie down the aisle. And of course his best man would be Joseph.

She assisted Claire into her wedding dress then went to the back of the hall to take her place. It dawned on her when she saw Joseph. He had realized that they would be paired up and didn't look forward to it. The hate was strong in him. But when he took one look at her, his heart melted and he had to keep reminding himself of why he hated her so much.

She took his offered arm without a word and they walked together up the aisle. Both were remembering another time, another day, when they stood together at Twin Oaks Plantation to become man and wife. It was an awkward time for both of them and neither one spoke.

Jennie remembered that the day was sunny with big puffy white clouds in the sky. Lois Miller had insisted that they get married at Twin Oaks and she had spared no expense for the wedding. The yard was decorated in long white ribbons. There was a gazebo where they would say their vows. A white runner led to the gazebo, a runner that would take her to the love of her life.

As Jennie walked on Hubert Miller's arm to where Joseph stood, she was the happiest person in the world. He looked so handsome in his white tux that it warmed her heart just to gaze at him.

She was dressed in a gown that was cut low in the front and had little puffed sleeves. The skirt was covered with ruffles and was wide enough to wear a hoop under it. Her hair was piled up on her head and she wore a diamond tiara that peeked out from the hair falling on her forehead.

Joseph thought that she was the most beautiful sight he had ever seen and even now as they walked up this aisle to see Michael and Claire wed, he could see her in his mind as she looked that day. That day that seemed as if it was in another lifetime. "Where did the two people go?" He wondered. "The two people who pledged their love, vowed to stay together in sickness and in health, till death parted them."

At the reception, Jennie had her usual flock of men suitors, and Chavez hovered around her like a mother hen. He didn't think any of these gangsters were good enough for his Jennie. He had sort of unofficially adopted her as his daughter, and he was never far from her side.

Jennie noticed that when Joseph danced with the bride, she was clinging to him as tightly as she herself used to cling to him and that made her angry. She knew she had no right, but that didn't make it any better.

She didn't know it but Joseph was watching her as she danced with each one of the guys, one after another. The green dress had affected him too, and he remembered the night when she was kidnapped.

"Joseph," Claire pouted, "your mind is a million miles away. What are you thinking about?"

Joseph didn't dare tell her that he was remembering another dance, a dance where he held Jennie in his arms. Where he lost himself in her hair, showered tiny kisses down her neck, and then found her lips.

"Joseph," she said petulantly, "are you listening to me?"

"What? Yeah, I'm listening."

"You were a million miles away," she said. "I'm jealous. Were you thinking about another girl?"

He just shrugged. He didn't even like Claire. He was trying to be polite for Michael's sake.

Just at that moment, Michael came up and said, "Joseph, this is my dance with my new wife and I believe you're supposed to dance with the Matron of Honor."

Joseph hadn't counted on that but didn't see how he could gracefully get out of it. He walked over to Jennie and said, "I believe it's the custom for the best man to dance with the Matron of Honor."

She came into his arms stiffly, nothing like she had done in the past. And it was just one more thing to prove to him how much she had loved Gary and how much she hated him for being the one who killed Gary.

There was no exchange of words, no nuzzling on her neck, just coldness between them. He spoke to break the awful silence. "Chavez hovers around you like a mother hen. Have you cast your spell on him too?" She tried to pull away from him but he held her tight. He was so full of hate that he felt like, now that he'd started, he couldn't stop saying what was on his mind. "Did you cast a spell on him pretty Jennie? Is he one of your victims too?" He saw the pain in her eyes but he couldn't stop. "I guess all your suitors will be fighting over you soon. They hang around you like a dog in heat."

She pulled back and slapped him across the face, causing his skin to weal up and turn red. He wanted to hit her back but knew everyone was watching them. Her face crumpled and she ran from the room crying. Joseph got drunk. Drunker than he ever had in his life.

When he finally quit drinking in the lounge and went to his suite, he sat on his bed and pulled his gun out. There was nothing to live for anymore. He had lost the only person in his entire life that he had allowed himself to love and for some reason, it was a forever love. He couldn't get out of it now that he had committed to it. And she would never love him again. He realized that now. He couldn't bear to continue in the lonely life that stared him in the face, the future without Jennie in it. Better to end it now than drag it out. This emptiness inside was killing him anyway. He might as well get it over with.

In his alcoholic muddle, he saw them, the demons in his room that watched with great expectation. They were joyful at the sight of this once powerful demon fighter sitting there with a gun in his hand to take his own life.

"Where's your strength now?" One of the demons jeered. "You don't look like anyone that we have to fear. I knew your God would desert you. He doesn't even send His angels to watch over you anymore."

Joseph cocked the gun and put it to his temple. One of the demons said to another one, "This one was easy. The girl will be easy too. We'll have them both destroyed then we'll get that next warrior of God and do away with him too!"

Even in a drunken stupor Joseph would not let them win. He fired the gun into the midst of them, casting them out in the Name of Jesus. "You won't win you vile creatures. Go back to hell where you came from."

T Ball came running into the room when he heard the shot. "Boss, you ok? What's goin on in here?"

"It's ok T Ball I'm just killin' a few demons. Don't worry, I'm not gonna kill myself, only the demons."

T Ball took the gun out of Joseph's hand. "Sure boss, you kill all those demons, but right now, why don't you just rest a while. Later we'll kill 'em together."

Joseph fell back on the bed mumbling, "I can't help it, I love her. I tried not to but it don't work. I can't stop the love and she don't love me."

"You go to sleep now boss. It'll all look better in the morning."

Jennie felt totally defeated. She could never win his love back. There was too much hate between them. And she didn't know how she could go on. She just didn't see any reason to live. She had lost her husband and her son. "What was there that was left to live for?" She wondered as she ran from the hall.

She entered the suite and headed for the bedroom. She took Gary's gun out of the drawer and cocked it. "Why should I continue in this life that I'm was trapped in?" She thought. "What's the point of going on?" She sat there holding the gun, trying to get the nerve to use it.

Chavez came into the suite and saw her sitting on the side of the bed, gun in hand. "No..." he shouted as he ran into her bedroom. "That's not the way out," he said as he took the gun from her hand. "Think about your son. What hope does he have without you?"

She put her face in her hands and cried, for her lost love, for her lost son, for her broken heart.

Everyone wondered what had happened between Jennie and the boss, but no one dared ask him. He was in a sour mood all the time now. He noticed however, that the men never mentioned Jennie anymore when he was around.

Joseph would have been even angrier had he known that one special suitor, Bradley Johnson was always hanging around, trying hard to get her attention. He bought little gifts for her and she tolerated his presence. Chavez didn't like him one bit, but it was Jennie's choice.

She consented to go to supper with him in the Casino dining room. He was a slick talker, blonde hair and blue eyes. Probably the resemblance to Joseph was what attracted her to him in the first place.

"Jennie, now that Gary's not around, you need a protector." He said. "I can make sure that all those guys hanging around you will disappear."

Jennie didn't answer. She drank the champagne in front of her and remembered Joseph holding her, Joseph always being there when she needed him. Even at night, so long ago, when Gary would drop her off after a day spent with him, Joseph would just show up. True, they usually said the wrong thing to each other and he would leave, but he would always come back.

"How about it Jennie?" He questioned. "You and I could be a number together."

Jennie remembered the night when Gary asked if she and Joseph were a number. So much water under the bridge, so many memories now flooding her mind that were once lost to her. "I'm sorry Bradley. I'm just not ready to make any commitments right now. I guess it's just too soon."

"Ok Jennie. I can wait. Just remember that I'm here for you if you need me."

She thought about Joseph, how he had always been there for her. How did she ever cope with life before Joseph? It just seemed like he was always there. Like there was no life before him. He talked about her putting a voodoo spell on him, it seemed just the opposite to her. She felt as if she were under his spell.

Bradley didn't know her well enough to notice how quiet she was. He just assumed that it was her personality. "But she sure is a looker," he thought. And Bradley liked to be seen with beautiful women. He realized that this was one woman he could really go for. He'd like to shower her with fancy gifts and take her to all the hot spots in Las Vegas.

"Can I call on you tomorrow?" He asked. "Maybe we can spend a day at the races. Ever been to the track here Jennie?"

She shook her head no. She was remembering another racetrack, a day she spent with Gary at the Fair Grounds in New Orleans. She certainly didn't miss Gary but she did miss New Orleans. It was the city of her birth, her home. All of her memories with Joseph were tied up there. And she was suddenly very homesick. She longed to return to New Orleans. She felt as if all of her ties were back there. And of course, if Joshua were still alive, he would be there. True, Joseph wouldn't be there, but this cold Joseph who hated her, was not the Joseph in her memories. And no one could ever take her memories from her.

"I have some things to do tomorrow," she finally answered, "but maybe in a day or two. Give me a call."

Bradley was disappointed but he knew that Jennie was not just another dame. He would have to take his time with her. She was a class act. He was used to hanging around with floozies, but his taste was changing. He liked the air of eloquence that rested on her. There was something about her, he didn't know what, but it made her different. Made her stand out from all the rest of the women he had known. "Ok love, I'll call you in a few days."

She hated it when someone called her "love". That was Joseph's pet name and it didn't sit well on anyone but him. She was his love, and he was her love. And she vowed to one day win his love again. He might hate her right now, but she could make him love her again. He was the only man she wanted. There could never be another relationship with a man. She might go to dinner with someone, like tonight. But there would never be that passion, that all consuming love that she felt for Joseph.

She let him bring her to her door, even let him kiss her good night. She hung limply in his arms. His kiss meant nothing to her. Only one person could arouse her, could put life back into her dead soul. And that person was Joseph.

Chavez had been listening for her return. He didn't like it at all that she was even having supper with this gangster. His Jennie was too pure, too sweet to hang around with the trash that was part of the mob. He was thankful to see that she came home early and that she was alone. He spent most of his time with her now. There were no romantic ties, just a fatherly love for her. There was just something about Jennie that he liked, and he vowed to be her protector. She was too delicate, too fragile to be hurt. Even by Joseph. So he vowed to even protect her from Joseph if need be. All of his loyalty was transferred to Jennie, the loyalty that had once been Michael's, and the loyalty that had once been Joseph's. He remembered his little daughter Antoinette, and found in Jennie everything that she would have been.

Joseph wallowed in his hate for her. She had hurt him more than any person in his life, including his mother and father. And when he found out that she had gone out with Bradley Johnson, his hate raged like a living thing, coursing through his body. He wanted a complete end of it so he filed for divorce.

Jennie had come to the point where she hated him for what he did to their child, even while she vowed to make him love her again. She wavered back and forth between hate and love. But then she'd always heard that there was a fine line between the two. However, when she got the divorce papers, she was livid with rage.

"Divorce?? He wants to divorce me? Of all the nerve..."

She went upstairs to his suite, and not even mindful of all the men sitting around, including Bradley, Jennie threw the divorce papers in his face. "You have your nerve. You're divorcing me after you signed our baby's death warrant. I hate you Joseph Hall. You're nothing more than a murderer! A murderer! A murderer!" She screamed at him as she began hitting him on the chest with her fists. All of her anger, her frustration was taken out on him now.

"What are you talking about Jennie? He asked as he grabbed her hands. What do you mean?"

"Gary had our baby. He said if I told you then he would have him murdered. And if he didn't check in with the people who have him, they would automatically kill him. And now he's dead because you killed Gary. Oh God, I want my baby back!" She crumpled against him in tears as he tried to digest this news.

"He lied to you Jennie, Lois Miller has Joshua."

"No," she moaned, "he was in a foster home and they can't find the foster parents or Joshua. Chavez has a private detective working on it."

"Sit down here, I'll call Lois. T Ball get her a drink to calm her down."

She took the glass but didn't drink any of it. The men in the room were amazed to find out that she was Joseph's wife. They each tried to remember what they had said about her in his presence and they all suddenly felt uncomfortable. Bradley felt the most uncomfortable. She was the boss's wife and he actually had aspirations of winning her over. He didn't know what to think about this situation. But it did give him hope to know that Joseph was divorcing her. "Maybe there's a way to win her after all." He thought.

"Lois, this is Joseph."

"Oh Joseph, thank God you called. I didn't know how to reach you. Joshua's gone. They can't find the foster parents who had him. They just took him and disappeared."

The blood drained from Joseph's face and he sat in a nearby chair because he was suddenly weak. "Ok, Lois. Thanks. I'll call you later."

Jennie stood up and faced him. "You can have your divorce. I'll never forgive you for being responsible for the death of our son." She spoke with a coldness Joseph had never felt from any woman before, and he knew he'd lost her forever.

Jennie left and Joseph was thinking; "Now it all makes sense. She put up with the beatings, the humiliation, anything Gary did to her for our son. And I only added to her misery. No wonder she hates me. I don't blame her, I hate myself."

Joseph went into his bedroom and closed the door, then he sat down and cried. He didn't care if it wasn't manly to cry. His whole life lay in ruins at his feet and he didn't know how to deal with it. He fell to his knees. "Oh God, if you're still with me, please help me. I've destroyed everything; lost my son, lost the only woman I'll ever love. Please help me." He cried this from a tormented soul and God took pity on him.

Suddenly the room was aglow with an un-earthly light, a light that Joseph remembered from a long ago past. "God has heard your prayer, Joseph," the angel said. He will strengthen you but you must bring Jennie back to the Lord. She doesn't remember that she is God's anointed. And you must find a way to reach her and bring her back to her calling." Then he was gone and somehow Joseph didn't feel very comforted.

"Reach Jennie?" He thought. "How will I ever break through the hate to reach her? She'll probably never even speak to me again and God knows I deserve that. Oh Jennie, what have I done?" He wept again, for his lost love, his lost son, his lost dreams. He had sunk as low as he could go in life and didn't know how he could ever right all the wrongs that he had caused. If ever he had wished for death, he longed for it now. He could only view death as a way out, a way to remove the pain that was in him like a living thing. If God wanted him on his face, wallowing in the dirt, then he'd arrived. If God wanted him to hit bottom, he was there. He didn't see how he could ever overcome this. This was too much to bear.

"God's warrior?" He thought. "That's really a joke. I can't control my own life, how could God ever think that I could cast demons out of people and get their life straight? How can I ever face Jennie again after causing our baby to die? How can I go on living now that I know what I've done. How can I even pretend to go forward in life? Oh Jennie," he cried from the depths of his soul. "How can you ever forgive me when I can never forgive myself. How can you, Oh God, even forgive me? I'm not worthy to be loved or forgiven by either one of you. But God help me. I don't want to live without her."

Chapter Nineteen

Joseph put off going to see Jennie because he was afraid. Afraid she wouldn't give him a chance to talk, afraid he had pushed her over the edge. He now knew that he had never hated her, he only hated what he thought she had done. And that was to fall in love with Gary. He loved her with everything in his being; he always had and always would. "Oh Jennie, my love," he thought, "what have I done to you?"

When he finally got up the nerve to go to her suite, he knocked and knocked but there was no answer. The housekeeper was coming down the hall so Joseph asked her if she could unlock the door. He was afraid she had done something foolish and he didn't have her key anymore. He had thrown it in the trash after that fateful day when he shot Gary.

"Sorry sir, but there's no one there anymore."

"What do you mean?" Joseph asked.

"They've moved. The suite is empty." She answered.

Joseph just turned and walked away. If God wanted him to hit bottom, then God had gotten His way. Because Joseph was at the end and didn't know what else to do, where to go from here.

He went to see Michael Rossi. "Do you know anything about Jennie moving out of the suite?" He asked.

"Yeah, she took my best man but I figured she needed somebody after all the poor girl's been through."

"What do you mean your best man?" Joseph asked, heart beating wildly. He had heard the rumor about Bradley hanging around her, taking her to supper. He couldn't bear to lose her to another man.

"I gave Chavez permission to go back to Louisiana with her. He's no good to me now. He's like a big puppy dog. His loyalty is to his new master and he's ruined for the old one."

Joseph felt weak in the legs with relief. "At least she didn't leave with Bradley Johnson," he thought. "And I'm glad she has Chavez. I know he'll take care of her." But then he thought, "How can I ever find her now? New Orleans is a big city."

"I have to go there," Joseph said. "I have to find her and our son."

"Ok Joseph, I'll tell you what. I'll let you go and run our New Orleans operation. I'll let the other guys down there know you're coming and that you're in charge. Will you do that?"

Joseph nodded. He would have agreed to anything at the moment. He just had to get back there. He had to find his love.

Joseph checked in with the ones running the New Orleans mob. He was surprised to find that they were set up in the Maison Blanche building on Canal Street, in offices that took up two whole floors. They were set up as a legitimate appearing business. There were many small businesses under them, all a cover up.

"Boy," Joseph thought, "I'd have a field day if I was still a cop."

He rented an apartment in the French Quarter for himself and T Ball. Michael Rossi had insisted that Joseph bring him along as a bodyguard. Joseph didn't feel the need for it but Michael insisted and Joseph gave in. There were still heads of other families who would love to see Joseph dead.

He combed the streets looking for her, showing her picture around, but no one knew her and no one had seen her. He went home discouraged every day.

He didn't even know how to begin looking for their son so he guessed he would just start at the beginning, the place he disappeared from. He went to Social Services and she gave him the last known address. "After all," he thought, "I wasn't a cop for nothing. I still know how to investigate."

At the address she had given him, there was a 'For Rent' sign on the door and it said apply next door. He knocked and waited while an elderly gray haired woman in a faded housecoat came to the door carrying a small dog.

"Hi," Joseph said. "I'm interested in the house next door. Wonder if I could look at it?"

"Well," the old woman said, "I'd have to get dressed."

"Madam I wouldn't think of putting you to any trouble. If you'll just give me the key I'll run look and bring it right back to you." He flashed her one of his smiles, dimples flashing at the corners of his mouth.

"Ok, I'll be right back. My what a nice man," she thought.

Once inside Joseph combed the place for something, anything, a clue to give him something to go on. He was about to leave in discouragement when he pulled open a drawer, and in the back stuck in a crack, was a business card with the name of an attorney on it. It might be nothing, but he hung on to it. The attorney was located in Biloxi Mississippi.

He went back to his apartment to check his messages, then shower, shave, and start out again. T Ball told him that Michael had called and it was very important. "And," T Ball said, "if you leave the apartment again I'll be with you. You snuck away this time but from now on I'm sticking to you like glue."

Joseph just laughed as he dialed the number. "Let me talk to Michael." He said as Claire answered the phone.

"Joseph!" She exclaimed. "You left without telling me. You bad boy you."

"Put Michael on," Joseph said flatly.

"Joseph? That you?" Michael asked.

"Yeah, it's me. What's goin' on?"

"You better find Jennie and warn her."

"Warn her? About what?" Joseph asked.

"Well you know we got men planted in some of the other families?"

"Yeah," Joseph said impatiently.

"One of them reported to me that they're looking for Jennie. When they find her they'll hold her to get to you. It's all out now about how she's your wife and all."

"Just great!" Joseph thought. "And these guys were good at finding people. What else could go wrong?" Aloud he said, "You don't happen to know where Chavez is staying, do you?"

"No, he hasn't been in touch since he left with her."

"Ok Michael, thanks." He still kept their relationship formal. He didn't think of him as a father and he would never call him anything except by his given name.

"T Ball, we've got our work cut out. Guys from the other families are coming here to look for Jennie. They want to use her to get to me. We've got to find her first. I just don't know where to begin."

"Boss you know that guys in the organization are top notch when it comes to finding people."

"Yeah, that's what I'm afraid of," Joseph said glumly.

"But my point is, we have plenty of Wiseguys down here that we could put to use." T Ball said.

"Hey, that's a great idea." Joseph said. "You go on down to the main headquarters and recruit some of them and put them to work. Here..." he handed him a few pictures of Jennie. "Give this to them to show around."

Chapter Twenty

Jennie was getting very discouraged. The private eye didn't have any new information and she didn't think she'd ever find her son. She and Chavez were living in an apartment on Esplanade Avenue, right out of the French Quarter.

In quiet times like today, more memories from the past were starting to come back. Chavez had gone to the grocery down the street to get the fixings for supper. She was remembering an angel visiting her. "What was it that he said?" She wondered. She couldn't bring up the words that he spoke but she was sure that she had had a visitation. She also remembered that she always used to pray to God and she felt like she needed to now.

She slipped down on her knees and prayed, "Lord, I don't remember anything about our relationship. I know I haven't even had a relationship with you lately, but if you'll forgive me, I'll try to get back to a right place with you. Help me Lord to find my son. In Jesus' Name, Amen.

Chavez returned and started supper. He was a man of many talents and Jennie was thankful to have him with her. He had insisted on coming and she was glad he did. When she thought about Joseph she realized that she had been hard on him. He had no way of knowing about Joshua. He had in fact thought Joshua was safe at Twin Oaks. She was sorry and would have liked to apologize, but she doubted if he would even speak to her again. And she doubted if she would ever see him again. When she thought about that, she felt like crying.

She tried not to let herself think about him holding her, kissing her. She longed for him in those moments when she couldn't stop the memories from coming. At one time, she had longed to remember every moment from the past, now she wished she could forget so the pain wouldn't be so real, so fresh. "Maybe I was better off when I had amnesia," she thought. "Some things are just too painful to remember."

And in these moments of remembering she continued to have a nagging feeling that something was there that had never returned to her memory, something that she should be remembering, but she couldn't seem to bring it out.

Jennie called Lois Miller to tell her she was back in town.

Lois was tickled to hear from her. "Jennie!" She exclaimed. "It's so good to hear your voice. Are you ok? How's Joseph?"

"I'm afraid I don't see Joseph any more Lois. He may have divorced me by now. But it's a long story."

"Oh no Jennie! How awful. You two were so in love and so meant for each other. Well you'll have to come out and visit and tell me all about it."

"Maybe later. Right now I have to stay close to here in case we find out anything about Joshua."

"Well I'll be praying for you and for Joshua. And Joseph," she added.

"Thanks Lois. I'll call you again sometime."

As she and Chavez were eating, someone crashed through the door and four men entered the room waving guns. Chavez went for his gun and they shot him. He fell to the floor and lay still, blood pouring from a hole in his stomach. Jennie screamed and tried to run to him but one of the men grabbed her by the arm and dragged her out of the room. They loaded her into a black SUV and drove off.

Joseph was sitting in Captain Parmeter's office when the call came in that neighbors reported a shooting on Esplanade Avenue. They said that the men who did the shooting were seen dragging a woman into a black SUV.

Joseph knew that it was a long shot, there were shootings all the time in New Orleans, but he asked the Captain if he could ride with him, just in case.

"So what have you been up to Joseph?" the Captain asked as they drove to the scene of the crime.

Joseph didn't want to tell him about his mob connections so he said, "I've just been hanging out here and there. Mostly looking for Jennie and the baby. You haven't gotten any leads on the baby's kidnapping, have you?"

"No, I'm afraid we can't find out anything. It's as if the foster parents have disappeared off the face of the earth. I sure am sorry Joseph. I thought you would have at least found Jennie by now."

"Yeah, I thought so too."

They pulled up to the apartment house on Esplanade and went up to the apartment where the victim still lay on the floor. Cops were swarming all over the place and the scene was so familiar to Joseph, he felt almost like he'd come home. He just wasn't cut out to be a mob boss. He was a cop.

When he walked into the kitchen and saw that it was Chavez, he broke out in a cold sweat and his mouth went dry. They loaded him onto a stretcher and were about to take him out of the room but Joseph stopped them. "Is he alive?" He asked.

"Yeah, just barely," the EMT answered.

Joseph turned to the Captain. "I know this man and he may know what happened to Jennie. Would it be ok if I rode to the hospital with him?"

"Sure Joseph. Let me know if you find out anything and we'll be along later to question him."

Jennie wanted to die on the spot. She couldn't go through any more of this. She felt as if her whole life was about kidnapping and murder. Like she was trapped in a nightmare with no way out. And Chavez... "Oh God, they shot him. Please let him live Lord."

The men had pulled her into the SUV, and then took off at dangerous speeds. It seemed like they drove forever. She couldn't figure out where they were, because they had blindfolded her when they put her in the car.

The vehicle finally stopped and she was dragged roughly up some stairs, stumbling all the way. She heard a door creak on its hinges and she was pulled into a room where they finally removed the blindfold. Four dark haired Italians were in the room and she saw a woman at the stove cooking something. The smell made her want to gag. Her stomach was not in the mood for food.

She was scared and she was nervous. And she was worried about Joseph. Because she knew that it was all about him. They would use her as bait to lure him in so they could kill him.

"Joseph," she cried in her mind. "Don't fall for it. Save yourself." She didn't care about her own life anymore. She had seen too much of life as it was. And it was always a nightmare. All the happiness, all the joy she remembered from the past, it was all gone. There was nothing left but this nightmare she was trapped in.

"Sit down and eat," one of the men told her.

"I'm not hungry," she answered.

"You'll get plenty hungry before this is finished. Better eat while you have the chance."

She toyed with the food on her plate. She took one bite and had to wash it down with water. She had no taste for food.

The apartment was neat and clean and she was surprised. You'd expect thugs to take you to a dingy, dirty hide-away. The woman who did the cooking didn't even look in her direction. No one spoke to her while she played with the food.

Finally, one of the men pulled her up from the table and put her into a bedroom that had a double bed, a chest of drawers, a nightstand with a lamp on it, and a small table in the corner.

"You'll sleep here. And I'll be watching you every second, so don't get any ideas."

Someone handed him a straight back chair and he sat facing the bed. She lay down on it but thought she could never sleep under the circumstances. However, she was fast asleep in minutes. The strain, the anxiety, had all worn on her body and she was more tired than she thought.

She had dreams, one after the other. The first one had her caught in a black swirling mist, then the mist cleared and she saw evil faces surrounding her. But in her dream, she felt a boldness come over her and she began casting out the evil in Jesus' Name and before long, it had disappeared and she stood there alone.

The second dream had her trapped again in the black swirling mist, but this time Joseph was there with her. As the mist lifted and the evil faces came toward them, Joseph began casting the evil out in Jesus' Name, and soon it disappeared right before their eyes.

When she awoke, she remembered the dreams but didn't understand what they meant. "Was this a lost memory from the deep recesses of my forgotten past," she wondered. "If so, what on earth could it mean?"

She slept again while her captor sat and watched her. But this dream was about her and Joseph dancing. Her subconscious always seemed to return to the memories that stood out in her mind, the happy memories she wanted to remember. As they danced, he kissed her hair, then showered tiny little kisses on her neck, until his lips found hers and they were lost in each other. Time ceased to exist; they reached the portals of heaven together.

Then suddenly, in the dream, she was standing on the dance floor all alone, and she felt an emptiness like she had never felt before. Joseph was lost to her and she didn't know how to get him back. "Oh Joseph," she whimpered in her sleep. "Come back to me my beloved."

Jennie woke up and would have cried if her captor were not sitting there watching her. But she wouldn't give them the satisfaction.

He was thinking about how beautiful she was and what a shame that it was wasted. He knew they would probably kill her along with Joseph. "What a waste," he thought.

Jennie had no concept of time. She didn't know if she'd been there for days or weeks. Time seemed to run together, become just a big blur. She lay in the bed all day until they brought her into the kitchen to eat. Then they put her back in the bed to sleep.

She welcomed the sleep because she would dream. And in her dreams she could escape the reality of life. She was once again with

Joseph; he was once again the love of her life. Over and over in her dreams she went over everything that had happened to them in the past, everything that happened before she was kidnapped, sometimes even before they were married.

She remembered riding in a car with Joseph and Gary, and Joseph's arm rested on the seat behind her. It seemed that every now and then he would lightly touch her shoulder and she would get tiny shivers, just at the pleasure of him touching her.

She dreamed that she was at Twin Oaks and Joseph was there playing with the kids on the floor. In her dream, they were their kids and Joshua was climbing on Joseph's back. They took Joshua upstairs to put him to bed and when she turned to go back into the room, she bumped into Joseph and he pulled her into his arms. "Joseph," she cried in her sleep, "where are you my love?"

Chapter Twenty-One

C havez didn't wake up in the ambulance and Joseph kept praying that he wouldn't die. Joseph knew who had Jennie. He knew it was one of the other families. He just wanted to find out which one by questioning Chavez. The other families, especially Joe Ditz, wanted him dead. Now they made sure he would turn himself over to them so they could kill him. Well, he once said he would die for Jennie if called upon to do it; now he would get the opportunity.

They arrived and Chavez was put in ICU. Joseph couldn't stay in the room with him but the nurse said she would let him know if Chavez woke up. He sat in the waiting room and prayed for God to protect Jennie. He guessed if he had to, he was ready to die. But he asked God to be able to hold Jennie once more and tell her how much he loved her. They had been through so much. The powers of darkness had kept them apart too long.

Chavez Corleone was a big man in Italy, the godfather of his village. He had minions working for him and he could get anything done that he chose. If someone got in his way, he would just have them "rubbed out". People respected his power and all came to him with their problems.

His wife Sarah and their little girl Antoinette were the center of his life, his real reason for living. Everything he did, everything he was, was to give them a better life than he'd had when he was growing up. Coming from very poor parents, he fought to get ahead and he had succeeded. By worldly standards, he had it all. And by the age of thirty, he was one of the most powerful men in his village.

Until the Mafia wars started in Italy. Young upstarts came along and challenged the authority of the other godfathers, seeking to take their place in the power scheme.

Chavez's wife and daughter were going on a day of shopping, a fun day together. The day was beautiful, sunny with a light breeze.

"Daddy," Antoinette said excitedly, "I'll bring you a surprise from town."

"What's my little princess going to bring me?" Chavez asked as he sat her on his knee.

"Well it won't be a surprise if I tell you." She put her little arms around his neck and kissed him. "You'll see daddy, you're gonna love it."

"I'll hold my breath until you get back," he laughed.

No body expected disaster to hit on a beautiful day as it was. But when their driver turned the key, the car exploded, killing his family, killing his dreams.

Chavez walked away from it all, the wealth, the power, the dreams. He took a boat to America and the first person he met was Michael Rossi.

Michael had heard his story and felt sorry for Chavez. He gave Chavez a job, and all of Chavez's love and loyalty was placed on Michael Rossi. It had bothered Michael in the beginning that Chavez was so tenderhearted, too much so to make a good mob man. But Chavez didn't let that stand in his way. He did whatever had to be done to protect Michael. And Michael found out that he was the one person that he could turn to with any problem. Chavez never betrayed a confidence or sat in judgment on Michael.

Now, years later as his life was hanging by a thread, his love and loyalty were to Jennie, who in Chavez's mind, was a replacement for his own lost little girl.

He stirred and began to awake from the drug-induced sleep. Oxygen flowed into his nostrils and he could hear the beat of his own heart from the monitor next to his bed. He wondered briefly where he was and what was happening, then it all came back to him and he attempted to get out of bed. The nurse fought to hold him down.

"Get me some help here," she shouted to the other nurses. "Send the orderly."

Joseph, right down the hall from the room, heard the commotion and ran to see what was happening. He assisted the nurse in holding Chavez down. "Whoa Chavez, hold still. You're ok and you're in the hospital."

"Jennie," he cried. "They got Jennie."

"It's ok," Joseph said. "We'll get her back, don't worry."

"Joseph?" He questioned.

"Yeah, it's me. You just rest and I'll handle it. Was it Joe Ditzs' men?"

"Yeah. Guess they want you pretty bad." He grabbed Joseph by the hand and said urgently, "Get her back Joseph. I lost my daughter years ago; I don't want to lose her too."

"I'll get her back Chavez. Somehow, I'll get her back. And when I do, I won't ever let her go again."

"I'm glad. You two belong together. If ever two people had a destiny together, you and Jennie do."

"I know. I lost that vision for a long time. But I won't ever lose it again."

"You be careful Joseph. These men are killers. They'd think nothing of making a deal to let her go then shooting both of you. They're devious men."

"I'll be careful. And Jennie and I will get through this somehow. With God's help, we'll make it."

Chapter Twenty-Two

Joseph called the Ditz family headquarters in Las Vegas and left a message for Joe Ditz to call him on his cell phone. In the meantime, he had arrangements to make.

His cell phone rang in a couple of hours with the call he was expecting. "Hello." Joseph said.

"Yeah, this is Joe Ditz. You wanted me to call."

"You have something of mine," Joseph replied.

"So... what do you offer in return?" Joe asked.

"Myself."

"When and where?" Joe asked.

"Tomorrow at noon. Toulouse Street wharf, pier 92."

Joseph stood on the pier, looking down at the swirling, muddy Mississippi River. "Is my life going to end here?" He thought. "God, please send your angels to help us and keep us safe. If Jennie and I truly have a destiny together, then this has to take place like I planned it."

Joseph didn't see them but four angels stood nearby watching the scene in front of them. Hundreds of demons were watching also with interest. They had tried for so long to get rid of these two; maybe today would be the day.

He saw the black SUV coming down the wharf and got nervous. He knew these men to be killers, and he didn't know if his plan would work or not. He prayed that he could hold Jennie one more time. "Please Lord; I just have to let her know how much I love her."

The car stopped and two men got out of the front, looked the area over and when satisfied, motioned for the men in back to get out of the car also. They had Jennie by the arms and pulled her roughly out of the car.

"Joseph, no," she whispered.

Joseph said to them, "Send her over here, and when she gets here, I'll come over there."

They let go of Jennie's arms and gave her a little push. She slowly walked in Joseph's direction. She felt as if she was walking the last mile to death row. She knew they would kill Joseph, probably her too. And her only regret was that she hadn't told him how much she loved him.

When she reached Joseph, she said, "No! You can't go to them. They'll kill you."

Joseph grabbed her arm and said, "Jump Jen!" He pulled her into the river with him.   Suddenly shots rang out from every direction as a swat team moved in and engaged the four men in a gun battle.

Joseph and Jennie surfaced and hung on to the ladder attached to the pier, as shots rang out above. He held on to her for dear life, her body crushed against his. "Oh God, Jennie, I thought I'd lost you again. Please don't ever leave me. I love you more than life itself."

"Oh Joseph!" She cried, "I love you too. Just hold me and don't ever let me go."

He pulled her to him and they kissed a kiss of longing for a love that had been lost, for all the time wasted.

Captain Parmeter looked down and said, "You two can come out of the water now. Or am I disturbing you?"

The large array of demons in the area were cursing and screaming when Joseph and Jennie made it out alive. They didn't want the two together, much less together and back in love with each other. Alone, each made a formidable foe, but when the two were united, the demons didn't have a chance.

"We separated them before and we can do it again," one of the demons shouted at the angels standing around as he shook his fist toward them. "You won't always be watching out for them. We'll get them again! And we've got their son, your so-called warrior of God. They won't ever find him. We'll make sure of that."

The angels flashed their swords toward the demons and they scattered, all the while cursing the angels, cursing Joseph and Jennie, and cursing God.

Chapter Twenty-Three

Jennie and Joseph stood over the hospital bed where Chavez lay. He looked more at peace now; his Jennie was safe. The doctor said he would recover but would need a lot of care at home. Jennie was willing and happy to provide it.

Chavez beamed when he looked at the two of them together. He'd known all along that they were meant for each other. "Boss I sure am glad you and Miss Jennie are ok. I was really worried about you two. Those thugs are killers and they probably wouldn't have let either one of you live."

Joseph laughed, "Not nearly as glad as we are to be ok. I didn't know if we'd get out of there alive, but old Captain Parmeter came through. The men are all in jail for kidnapping. I guess Michael will get some backlash from this."

Chavez nodded. "Yeah, guess you better call and warn him."

Joseph nodded and flipped open the cell phone to call Michael. It was, after all, his obligation to warn him. Michael had really, in his own way been good to Joseph.

Jennie told Chavez, "You need to think about yourself now Chavez. We need you to get well enough to come home so we can take care of you for a change. And no more of this 'Miss Jennie' stuff. Just call me Jennie."

He smiled at Jennie. "Is tomorrow soon enough Jennie?"

They brought Chavez home from the hospital and got him settled in his bedroom with orders to call if he needed anything. Joseph and

Jennie were anxious to be alone. There didn't seem to be enough hours in the day for him to hold her and kiss her. He wanted to make up for all the time they had wasted.

Chavez recovered in record time and they knew it was time to put their efforts into finding their baby. They now both knew that God had them together for a destiny and that they would one day have Joshua again. They just chafed at all the time wasted. He was getting bigger and they weren't with him to see it. And Jennie had not even held him and her arms ached to hold her baby close to her, to feel his heart beating with her own.

One night as they lay quietly in bed, Joseph said, "Jennie, do you remember the first time we met, that night at Twin Oaks Plantation when you came there to help Lois' son Aubrey?"

"Just vaguely. I had a dream one night and we were sitting in a room with a lot of ancestors' pictures hanging on the wall. That's all I remember." Then she added, "But I did have a weird dream one night. I was surrounded by that same black mist, and when the mist went away, I saw the evil faces surrounding me. But I wasn't scared. I started saying, 'in Jesus' Name I cast you out', and they disappeared. Then I dreamed the same dream but you were there and you were the one who cast them out in Jesus' Name."

"Jennie, God is trying to remind you of who you are and what He has for us to do."

"What do you mean?" She asked, puzzled.

"When I met you, you were a deliverer, a demon fighter. You used to see demons and angels all over the place and you had a big ministry in the French Quarter casting demons out of people. That's what you were doing at Twin Oaks, casting demons out of Aubrey Miller."

She was amazed at this revelation yet she felt like the mist was starting to dissolve more and she could actually see some of the lost memories. She remembered sitting on Joseph's lap, attempting to get up when a large demon threw her across the room.

"I do remember a little now that you mention it. A demon threw me across the room and I hit my head."

"Yeah, that's when you got amnesia."

"You know," she said, "I used to see these black figures following Gary around, sometimes they were all over him. I thought it was the drugs he was giving me."

"You were seeing into the Spiritual realm Jennie. God wants you to remember all of this because He's not finished with us yet. Do you remember that the angel told me that Joshua would be a warrior of God?"

"Now I do!" She exclaimed. "And we need to thwart the devil's plans and get Joshua back. He has a destiny too."

"We will, my precious. Somehow we'll find him and the three of us will be God's warriors again. I don't want to say too much at once. Just digest what we've talked about and we'll talk more as time goes on. God told me that I was to bring you back from where you had gone astray, that I was to bring to your remembrance all that He had called you for."

The next morning as they were sitting down to breakfast, Joseph's cell phone rang and T Ball shouted, "Get out...get out now. The Ditz family is coming to get you all."

Joseph looked out the window. "They're here—Chavez, get her outta here."

"No, I won't leave you again." She cried.

"Go underground. I'll find you. Go—now. Get her outta here now, Chavez." Joseph shouted.

Chavez grabbed her and dragged her out of the back door of the apartment. "He'll be ok," he said.

They heard shots ringing out as they ran.

"Joseph!" she screamed. "Joseph..." This last was wrung out of her in anguish.

Chavez pulled her down the back steps and into the street. He kept going until they couldn't hear any shots or see her apartment house any more.

"Where can we go?" he asked.

"I don't know, I can't think... wait, head another street over. I have a friend who lives there. She'll help us."

They came to her friend's apartment building and knocked on the door. Alicia opened the door and saw Jennie looking frantic. "Come in, what's wrong?" She asked.

"We need a place to stay. Somewhere safe." Jennie answered.

"You can stay here for now, and after dark I'll take you both someplace else, someplace safe where no one will find you." Alicia said. She didn't even question Jennie about what kind of trouble she was in. Jennie had delivered her of many demons and she was a different person, thanks to Jennie. She'd do all she could to help them.

"Oh God, please not again." Jennie cried in her mind. "I can't lose him again. I can't go through this again. Help us, please help us."

When it was dark Alicia led them from her apartment, and they headed for the safe place she had referred to. They walked for several blocks then Alicia turned into a small alleyway and up a flight of stairs leading to a balcony apartment. She entered the apartment, with them following. Once inside, Alicia pulled up a rug that was lying on the floor. Below the rug was a trap door with stairs leading downstairs into another apartment.

"This was an underground slave house." Alicia said. "No one will find you here. The apartment belongs to a friend who's in France, so you'll be all alone. I'll replace the rug. If you should hear sounds from upstairs, just keep quiet. If it's me, I'll knock three times on the trap door before I open it. But I won't come back unless I absolutely have to. There's plenty of food. My friend keeps it stocked just in case. You never know when someone will need to hide out."

"Alicia," Jennie said, "if you hear anything concerning me, please find out all you can and let us know."

"Sure Jennie. If I hear anything, like I said, I'll knock three times."

Alicia left and Jennie sat down, put her face in her hands, and sobbed. "Oh Joseph," she cried. "Please find me. Please God, keep him safe."

Chavez just patted her on the shoulder. He didn't know what else to do. She had been through so much; his heart broke for her.

Joseph had his hands full. Shots were ringing out and bullets were zinging past his ears. But at least Jennie was safe. He dialed 911 on his phone and prayed he could hold out until they got there. He was crouched behind the L shaped counter in the kitchen.

A bullet caught him in the arm and he dropped his gun. He quickly fumbled around until he felt it and resumed shooting at the assailants. A short time later, he heard sirens and the shots ceased. He slipped down the back steps, blood flowing down his arm. He didn't know where to go so he called T Ball to meet him on Bourbon Street, down past all the clubs where it was isolated and quiet.

T Ball found Joseph, took off his jacket, and wrapped it around his arm. "We gotta find a place to go boss. We gotta get off the street."

"Yeah, I know. Let me think... I know a stripper who lives near here. We'll go there."

They entered a back alley behind the Jazz club. Joseph knocked on a door and a woman's voice asked, "Who's there?"

"Joseph Hall."

She opened the door and told them to come in. "You're bleeding!" She exclaimed.

She quickly got some towels, scissors and peroxide. She cut the sleeve from his shirt exposing his bloody arm. Hold your arm over the towels Joseph so I can clean the wound. She poured the peroxide and he winced. She felt around the wound and said, "I don't feel the bullet, at least I'm assuming that's what it was."

Joseph nodded.

"It must have gone clear through. If it doesn't get infected, it should be ok." She wrapped a piece of sheet around the wound and made a sling for his arm.

"Candi, this is T Ball, a friend of mine."

"Hello T Ball. Never a dull moment when you hang around with Joseph, is there?" She spoke as someone who knew him well.

"How did you find out?" Joseph asked T Ball.

"Michael called. He has good loyal men planted in the Ditz family. He usually finds out everything they do. He said they're plenty mad since you sent four of their best men to jail for kidnapping. I don't think they'll leave you alone Joseph."

Joseph ran his hand through his hair nervously. "At least Jennie's safe."

"Who's Jennie?" Candi asked.

"She's my wife, Candi."

"You? You tied the knot? Well you could knock me over with a feather. She must be mighty special for the ice man to fall for her."

"She is," he grinned. "She's the most special person I've ever met. Listen Candi, how does a person go about finding someone who went underground to hide?"

"By underground you mean that someone from the Quarter hid her?"

"Yeah. And I have to find her."

"I'll be leaving for work soon. I'll ask around, discretely of course. She must really be special," she laughed. "You guys had anything to eat today?"

"No," they said in unison. Joseph added, "And we could sure use something. Got anything?"

"Yeah, I've got some pot roast left over from last night. I'll warm it for you before I get dressed to leave."

Chapter Twenty-Four

C andi Brewster was a slim girl with long brown hair, hazel eyes, and a heart of gold. Candi was not her real name, but her stage name. She was actually born Virginia Brewster in uptown New Orleans, that area where the elite lived, called the Garden District.

And Virginia was of the upper crust. Her parents were heirs and owners of the famous Dixie Brewery in New Orleans. Old money, old charm. But Virginia always had a wild streak and couldn't conform to cotillions and fancy parties.

She started rebelling when she was twelve years old and her parents caught her in the garage smoking with a young boy who lived in another neighborhood; an area of little shotgun houses, paid workers at Dixie Brewery.

And although they set their goals high for her, she had other ideas. At her coming out ball at sixteen, she invited the same boy she had been caught smoking with, and the two of them spiked the punch. It wasn't known until half of the debutante ladies were drunk. Her parents were mortified, unable to face their social elite circles and they had to take an extended cruise to Europe or face social ruin. No one was willing to invite their wild daughter to their events.

When she reached eighteen, she could no longer pretend to conform to the lifestyle they had chosen for her so she just quit pretending. She moved to the French Quarter and took a job as a stripper. Her family immediately disowned her. And now, at twenty-seven, she continued in the lifestyle that she had chosen.

She had met Joseph when one of her customers got too rowdy and started beating her up. He had been buying her drinks that was supposed to be champagne, but was really white grape juice. The owner of the club called the cops and Joseph was one of them sent to investigate. That was when he was a cop on the beat, before his move to vice.

He liked Candi and they began dating. It was one of the romances where he really would have liked to fall in love with her, but something in him held back.

She once screamed in his face, "You really are made of ice! You have no emotions and don't know how to love!" And at the time, he totally agreed with her.

The romance subsided when they both drifted toward others. But they remained good friends through the years. And she really had a soft spot for Joseph in her heart because he had been her first true love.

Jennie was afraid to call his cell phone; afraid the mob would trace her call and find out where she and Chavez were staying. This was a perfect hideout and she would have been content to stay here if only Joseph had been with her. But she didn't know if he was even alive, and that's what worried her. All she could do was to lie low and wait for her friend Alicia to ask around, to find out something.

She slept fitfully, one minute her arms longed to feel Joseph in them, the next she longed to hold her baby boy. She dreamed again that she was casting demons out, this time it was a young girl. The girl had been raised in a cult, and they made her perform all sorts of satanic practices. She came to Jennie for help and Jennie cast demons out. Then in the dream, she remembered a spirit called python that came to her and started squeezing the life out of her. He was hard to cast out but eventually he turned her loose because of the Name of Jesus.

When she awoke in the morning, she felt as if she had been doing battle all night, just remembering it all. While Chavez fixed breakfast, she heard three taps on the trap door and knew it was Alicia.

She came down the stairs and Jennie figured that she had news or she wouldn't have come back. Jennie felt faint. She was afraid that the news might be bad.

"I spoke to a girl I work with, one I know I can trust, and she had some news about what happened Jennie."

Jennie's mouth was suddenly dry and the palms of her hands were sweaty. Her heart was beating loudly, so loudly she thought they must surely hear it. "And?" She questioned.

"Do you know a guy named Joseph?"

Jennie could only nod. Her voice wouldn't work.

"It seems that he was shot."

Chavez caught Jennie before she hit the floor.

He put wet rags on her head and slapped her hand. "Wake up Miss Jennie, wake up."

She tried to focus on Chavez through the mist of darkness that had engulfed her once more. Then she sat up straight as she remembered the words of Alicia. "Is he dead?" She asked glumly.

"No, a girl named Candi took care of the wound. I think she's an old girlfriend."

"Thank God he's alive." She thought. "Never mind who took care of him. I'm just grateful that he's still on this earth with me." Aloud she said, "Alicia, could you take us to this girl's house?"

"Yeah, I know where she lives but we'll have to wait until it gets dark. I don't have to be at work until nine tonight so I'll come back around seven thirty and get you two."

Jennie just nodded, too choked up to talk.

The day seemed to drag on forever. Finally, it was time for Alicia to arrive and she heard three taps then saw Alicia coming down the stairs.

"Ya'll ready?" She asked.

They nodded and followed her up the stairs. It was dark upstairs but Alicia had a flashlight. They walked for a few blocks and finally Alicia turned into an alleyway behind the Jazz club.

Jennie knew this area well, she was starting to remember coming to apartments to cast out demons and minister to strippers and street people. "How could I have forgotten such an important part of my life?" She wondered. Then she realized that the forces of darkness probably helped her forget.

Alicia knocked on a door that opened shortly. They went in and when Joseph and Jennie saw each other, everyone in the room seemed to disappear as she ran into his arms. She held him so tight that it caused his arm to bleed again, but he didn't care. He welcomed her embrace. He buried his face in her hair and breathed in her scent. This is where he would always belong. No matter where they went, or what life had to offer, he was ok as long as he could hold her in his arms. He whispered her name, "Jennie... my love."

Jennie cried with relief to know he was ok. "Oh Joseph, I thought I'd lost you again."

"You won't ever lose me again. I promise you love; I'll always be here for you. I seem to always be saying that but I'll keep my promise to you this time. I don't want anything to ever come between us again. I guess I love you with a forever love, and there's no way out. You're stuck with me for life, I'm afraid." He kissed her and they were lost in each other.

Those in the room were a little embarrassed at the love exchange taking place. Candi felt a twinge of jealousy. After all, at one time she had wanted him to love her that way.

Joseph was suddenly aware of the others in the room. "Jennie, this is Candi, a good friend of mine."

Jennie looked at him and raised one eyebrow. He knew that she was remembering when he told Gary that she was just a good friend, and he smiled and whispered in her ear as he pulled her to him, "Not like you're thinking."

"Candi," Jennie said, "thank you so much for helping Joseph."

"I was glad to help," she replied. "After all, I knew you had to be very special to hook Joseph Hall in Holy Matrimony." She laughed.

Jennie laughed as she thought, "I could become friends with her very easily."

Chapter Twenty-Five

Joseph, Jennie, T Ball, and Chavez left to go back to the slave apartment where they thought they would be safer. As they all sat in the living room drinking coffee, Joseph hit her with a bombshell.

"Jennie I have to go back."

"Back, back where?"

"To Las Vegas," he answered.

"Oh no, Joseph, they'll kill you for sure."

Joseph said with emotion, "I can't let this keep dragging on. We have to get free so we won't have to look over our shoulders all the time."

"Then I'm going with you," she stated with finality.

"Oh no you're not," he said quickly. "And now the subject is closed."

She stood up and faced him with her hands on her hips. "If you think you'll go anyplace without me Joseph Hall, you're sadly mistaken. I had my baby ripped from my womb, I endured beatings and humiliations, I lost your love and lived trapped in a nightmare. If you go back, then I'll be right by your side. If they kill you, then life wouldn't be worth living anymore. I'd want to die too."

He smiled. He knew she had won. He noticed T Ball and Chavez grinning from ear to ear.

They got off the plane in Las Vegas, and Jennie humbly thanked God that this time she was with her beloved Joseph. Michael Rossi had sent a car for them and they went straight to the Blackjack. He even had Joseph's suite clean and ready for them. They showered and changed before they were to meet with Michael.

They sat in his penthouse and Joseph said, "Michael, I have to call a meeting of all the families, including the Ditz family. I have to get this thing settled. We can't go on running from his men."

"Ok Joseph, do what you think is best. But I hope you have a good plan because they don't give up easily."

Joseph sent out invitations for a large party being thrown in Michael Rossi's honor. He signed it Claire Rossi. He didn't want them to know just yet that he was back, or that he was exercising authority.

He reserved the banquet hall and planned the menu. He wanted it to be extravagant, no expense spared. In the center of one of the long tables would be an ice sculpture in the shape of a large angel. He figured he needed all the angels he could get to be there.

On the day of the dinner, he and Jennie prayed together and asked God's angels to be there. And asked for God's grace upon them. They bound the demons in the area, and bound them at the door of the hall. They didn't want any outside help against them.

Jennie was stunning in a white dress that hugged her figure, had a high neckline but a backless back. She piled her hair on top of her head and let one stray piece rest gently against her cheek. Joseph was again reminded of the night he saw her in the Casino with Gary, but the bitterness wasn't there anymore. He just remembered how her beauty struck him. And tonight he almost felt an awe for her. She looked pure in the white dress in spite of its revealing curves against her body. She looked like God's anointed again. He could almost swear there was a light around her, a holy glow.

There were surprised looks on all of the guests, especially from the other families. The Ditz family had shown up. They didn't know that Joseph would be there.

Dinner progressed and glasses clinked as drinks were handed out by the waiters. Joseph noticed that since they had bound the demons, there was not an attitude of dissent in the room, but almost a cordial presence.

As dessert was being served, Joseph stood and hit his glass with a fork to get their attention. He remembered a night so long ago; it seemed like another lifetime, when Michael had done the same thing to introduce him.

All attention was on him and he silently prayed for strength and grace. "Welcome my friends. It's an honor to have you all present. This dinner is to honor Michael Rossi, but it is also to honor all of you as his friends. I know some of you go way back with Michael."

The older ones were nodding their heads. They did have some good memories of their younger days together when they were just establishing the organization, setting up the mob.

Joseph continued, "So tonight I wanted to say that I am grateful to all of you for including me in your family. But I find that I cannot continue as second in command in the Michael Rossi organization."

"What?" Michael rose in surprise. "What are you talking about Joseph?"

He held his hands out to have them calm down so he could explain. "I am honored to have been chosen in the role Michael placed on me. But my heart is not in it as your hearts are. So I'm proposing an alliance between the Ditz family and the Rossi's. You all seem to have forgotten that you were once good friends. You can have that again and work together for the organization."

Michael Rossi was stunned. But he secretly admired Joseph for his finesse. An alliance would certainly keep them off his back.

Joe Ditz stood up and shouted above the din, "What does Michael Rossi think about this? All we've heard is his son's words."

Michael stood up. "My son is wise. Even in my youth, I could not have shown such wisdom as he's shown here tonight. And I bow to his wisdom. I'm willing to give it a try if you and your family are willing."

The Ditz family could do nothing but agree. The matter was settled.

Chapter Twenty-Six

A s Joseph stood on the balcony looking down at the pool, Jennie came up behind him and put her arms around his waist. She rested her cheek against his back. It was so good to have him back in her arms. "You were wonderful tonight. God must have really anointed you with that speech."

He grinned as he turned and faced her. His arms pulled her to him. "You inspired me, my little holy one. When I looked at you tonight, you seemed to glow with a holy glow. And I knew that you were once again God's anointed, His beloved. And my beloved." He kissed her deeply. "Jennie," he whispered. "My Jennie. I never thought I could love someone so completely. I begrudge all the years before I met you. God should have let us meet when we were little so we wouldn't have wasted any time."

She laughed. "I can just see us now, little Jennie and little Joseph making mud cakes together."

They laughed, and then they both got quiet as they looked out over the beauty of the heavens. The sky was radiant with stars and they marveled at God's creation. They had been through so much, but Jennie knew that it made stronger Christians out of them. She remembered the Lord telling her years ago that all she endured when she was growing up made her she person she had become. And she guessed that God must have a lot of work for them because He sure let them go through a lot.

She thought about Joshua and she started crying softly.

"What is it love?" Joseph asked.

"Oh Joseph, my arms ache to hold my baby. I've been denied the greatest gift a mother can have and that's to hold her newborn child. I know that we are in God's plan and that everything we went through made us stronger people, but that's my one regret: one that can't be undone."

His heart broke for her as he tightened his arms around her. He could understand some of how she felt because through all of the trials, his greatest desire had always been to hold her in his arms. Although he couldn't relate to that mother love thing, he could relate it to his love for her.

"We'll find him love. God won't let us down. He's meant to be with us and be raised as God's deliverer. Now that all of this other stuff is settled and nobody's chasing after us, we can put all of our attention to finding our son."

"But Joseph, we don't even have a clue where to start. How will we. . ."

"Hold on a minute," he interrupted her. "I just remembered something. I searched the place where the foster parents lived and found a card." He dug through his wallet. "Yes, here it is. Carl Jensen, Attorney at Law, in Biloxi Mississippi. That's where we'll start our search."

They flew back to New Orleans to take care of business there before heading to Biloxi. Chavez had insisted on coming back with them. He was still their bodyguard, and their bodyguard he would remain.

They gave up the apartment that Joseph and T Ball had been staying in, and kept the one on Esplanade. It was roomier with two large bedrooms and a good-sized living room, kitchen combination. The living room had windows across the front making it light and cheery. They had lost the apartment that she and Joseph lived in before she was kidnapped, so this was the next best thing.

Joseph told her, "Jennie, we've got to play this cool. We don't want to just run off to Biloxi guns waving, so to speak."

"What do you mean?" Jennie asked.

"I'm going this morning to talk to Captain Parmeter and see if I can get a make on this attorney. Maybe something will turn up in the police files."

Joseph sat in a chair facing Captain Parmeter. "Captain, have you heard anything about an attorney named Carl Jensen in Biloxi Mississippi?"

"No," he replied. "The name doesn't sound familiar but let me pull up the National Database and see if we find anything." He pulled it up on his computer and typed in the name Jensen. There were a lot of Jensen's that came on the screen so he narrowed the search by putting in the first name. A file popped up attached to the name Carl Jensen.

"Yeah," the Captain said, "he's in here all right. Looks like he's one of those shady adoption lawyers who do adoptions on black market babies."

"How does that work?" Joseph asked.

"Well someone sells him a baby that's either been stolen, or some crack mom doesn't want anymore. He advertises in all the newspapers in the south that he's looking for a good couple to adopt the child. And of course he charges them a whopping sum for the adoption. What it amounts to is they're selling babies."

Joseph felt his heart sink. Joshua could be any place by now.

"You know," the captain continued, "this is a pretty good lead on the kidnapping of your son." He opened his desk drawer, pulled out a gun and badge, and laid them on the desk. "I could use a good cop to investigate it."

Joseph smiled. It was good to be back. "Thanks Captain. I'll get right on it."

They checked into the Lucky Aces hotel in Biloxi. They chose this place because Michael Rossi owned an interest in it and he recommended it when Joseph had spoken to him earlier. They registered for two suites. One for them and one for Chavez. Since

Michael was picking up the tab they figured they might as well splurge.

It was a magnificent structure on the beach overlooking the Gulf of Mexico. Gentle waves lapped at the sandy shore as people sunbathed or frolicked in the water. A light breeze blew across the city, bringing with it the scent of salt water.

Their suite was decorated in a jungle motif and the bedroom had a massive king size bed with a tester top, reminiscent of the beds at Twin Oaks Plantation. Jennie thought back to those days, the weekend she first met Joseph, and she marveled at all that had gone on since then. "We were so naive then," she thought. "It seems like a million years ago."

She remembered the first time she saw him. He was so handsome in a blue sports jacket, blue matching pants, and a white shirt open at the neck. They were both at the Miller's Plantation home for the weekend and she was there to cast demons out of Aubrey, the four-year-old son of the Millers. She remembered every detail now, memories that a short while ago were locked in her subconscious, and she was unable to recall them.

She was God's anointed, what did Joseph call her that first weekend? "Demon buster". She laughed with the remembrance. So long ago, but time had only caused their love to deepen, to become a consuming love for each other. "Lord, I couldn't live without him," she thought. "He is part of me, flesh of my flesh."

She, Joseph, and Chavez sat down to supper in their suite and made plans. They had ordered it sent up and the food was before them on the dining room table. Succulent lobster, crab cakes, fried shrimp, gumbo, and stuffed crabs were spread out before them.

Chavez was not sure he was too keen on this seafood stuff but had agreed to try it. "I'll eat anything that doesn't try to bite me back," he said laughing.

"Well Joseph," Jennie said, "do you have a plan?"

"Yes, actually I do," he answered. "You're going to get a job."

"What?" She asked, surprised. "Me get a job?"

"Yeah, I talked to a friend of Michael's here in town and he said he could arrange for you to work at a small diner on Main Street, down in the city away from the beach area. That way you can discreetly ask if anybody had adopted a baby in the last year. In the meantime, Chavez and I will question the attorney."

"Oh Joseph, do you think it's wise? What if he gets scared and warns someone to skip town with Joshua?"

"Don't worry; I know how to handle these things. He won't get on to us."

"Ok, when do I start my new job?" She asked while struggling to get the shell off the lobster.

"Tomorrow morning. You'll go to the diner and say that Johnny Diaz sent you. The owner already knows you're coming."

Chapter Twenty-Seven

Jennie caught a cab to the address Joseph had given her and went into the diner. The main street was just a short street with a few businesses on it. There was a laundry mat, the diner, a small furniture store, a drugstore, and a variety store at the corner. It looked like a scene from mid-America in a magazine. Time had not caught up with this area. It was still locked into the past, in the time frame before the beach area had taken over the city with its Casinos and tourist attractions.

Jennie asked for the owner and a short chubby man came out from the kitchen area.

"I'm Jennie. Johnny Diaz said you have a job for me."

"Yeah, get a uniform from Mattie over there and she'll show you what to do."

Mattie was a tall girl with short blonde hair and a few freckles scattered across her nose. She had a pink uniform on with a white apron over it. She took Jennie into the back and showed her a set of lockers. She then went to a closet that held different sizes of uniforms and asked Jennie what size she was. She pulled it from the hanger and showed Jennie to a bathroom to change.

It wasn't the most flattering outfit that Jennie had ever worn, but it was modest and she was thankful for that. She put the apron over the uniform and went out to join Mattie.

Mattie showed her where everything was; how she had to fill sugar, salt and pepper shakers each morning, make sure everything was clean and in order for the breakfast crowd. Then after breakfast, they would prepare for the lunch crowd.

"We do a pretty good business here at times," Mattie said. "It just depends on whether or not the old townspeople feel like eating out. We don't get much tourist trade. Just home folks."

The day went quickly for Jennie because she had a lot to learn and she was kept busy all day. There wasn't much time for conversation but Mattie assured her that it wasn't like this all the time. She would get some days when she'd be bored to death because it was so slow.

She was tired at the end of the day but she looked forward to snuggling in Joseph's arms. That made the whole day worthwhile.

Joseph sat in the office of attorney Carl Jensen. They had decided that Chavez should wait in the car and if he saw or heard anything, he could warn Joseph.

Carl was a greasy looking little fellow with a black, pencil thin moustache, slicked back hair, and a gold crown on his front tooth. He wore a three-piece grey suit and expensive alligator shoes.

"Well Mr. Brown, what can I do for you today?" He asked.

"My niece had a baby out of wedlock and I thought you could help me locate the child. There's a huge reward for whoever finds him. I mean really huge." Joseph said.

"How huge are we talking?" Carl asked.

Joseph could see the greed all over his face. He also saw demons hanging around the office. "Two hundred grand." He answered casually.

Carl's eyes widened. "You're willing to pay that kind of money to get a baby back? And just why did you come to me? Why do you think I can help?"

Joseph looked around the room and leaned in toward Carl in a conspiratorial way. "It's not really my niece. I'm connected to the mob in Las Vegas and they got in touch with the local mob here. Your name came up. Actually, there's a substantial reward on the child. So I'm willing to offer you a two hundred grand finder's fee." Joseph winked at him.

He handed Joseph a tablet and pen. "Write down any information you have on the child, its mother, etc. Also, put your phone number where I can reach you. I'll check around and get back to you."

When Joseph had left the office, Carl dialed a number and when someone answered he said, "I think they're here. At least I'm pretty sure it's them. What do you want me to do?"

Joseph left there with an uneasy feeling. Maybe it was seeing all the demons hovering around, but the feeling persisted. He didn't want to worry Jennie so he didn't say anything. With so much demonic activity around he was afraid the devil would blow their cover or cause whoever had Joshua to flee the area.

"Lord please send your angels to help us find Joshua. Father, it's been a year now and Jennie hasn't even held him. Please Lord, please help us."

Joseph didn't see them but there were indeed angels all around him and Jennie. "Are we close to the end of this now?" one of the angels asked another. "Are they going to get the child back now?"

"Only the Father knows. But everything that happens to these two is in His plan, so it's always for their good."

Jennie went back to work the next day, and sure enough, business was slow and the day dragged on and seemed to last forever. "I'm sure thankful I don't really have to do this for a living," she thought.

She and Mattie sat around talking while the owner scrubbed the grill in the kitchen. "So are you from here Mattie?" Jennie asked.

"Yeah, I grew up here and guess I'm stuck for the duration. I don't have enough money or talent to go anywhere."

"I had a niece who lived here once," Jennie said. "That was about a year ago."

"Really? What was her name?" Mattie asked.

"Loretta Maiford. She was pregnant and left home to have her baby so no one would know she got pregnant out of wedlock. I think she gave it to a family that lived around here. She had a little boy."

Mattie shook her head. "I don't know of anybody around here adopting a baby boy. Where did you say you're from?" Mattie asked.

"Las Vegas," Jennie answered. "I worked out there but you know; everything gets old after a while. I'm heading to Florida to see if there's anything there for me."

"You know," Mattie said, "I think I did hear of someone who adopted a baby. I'll call my sister. She would remember."

She went into the back to call her sister and Jennie waited, all the while praying. "Please God, just let us find him. He's such a little fellow and he needs me. Oh Lord, I need him."

Mattie came back smiling. My sister knows exactly where the couple lives. She'll pick you up and take you there. Change your clothes and I'll watch for her."

Jennie had an uneasy feeling about going off with someone without telling Joseph but if they were to find their baby, she would just have to do whatever she had to do.

Shortly a pleasant looking woman probably in her mid thirties came into the diner and Jennie went out to the car with her. She made small talk on the way. "I'm Flossie, Mattie's sister. I know the couple you're talking about and I bet you'll be glad to see your nephew. You'll see that he has a good home and good adoptive parents."

Jennie realized that she had left her purse in the locker, but she could always get it later.

They drove up to a yellow frame house. The yard was neatly tended and there were flowerbeds across the front as well as around each tree. Blue curtains hung in the front windows, moving occasionally to the breeze blowing in from the water, three blocks away.

Jennie's heart was pounding so hard it felt like it would come out of her chest. She got out of the car and went inside with the woman. "Have a seat," the woman said. "I'll be right back."

She returned shortly holding a baby and Jennie thought she was going to cry. He was a tiny miniature of Joseph. She had found Joshua.

Jennie stood up to take the baby, when she noticed out of the corner of her eye that a man had entered the room. When she turned to look at him, all the color drained from her face, and she felt that familiar blackness overcoming her as she fainted.

When she came to she was lying in a bed, and her hands and feet were tied. The rope to her hands was extended to the head of the bed and she couldn't move. "Oh no," she thought, "not again. How could that have been Gary? I saw him killed right before my eyes."

She didn't have long to wait for an answer. The man entered the room. He looked just like Gary but he was a little chunkier, and minus the goatee and moustache. "Gary?" She questioned.

"No, actually I'm Jack. But you must be Jennie."

She was totally confused, and he saw it in her eyes and laughed. "You really thought I was Gary at first, didn't you? And just the fact that you fainted when you saw me tells me that Gary must be dead, right?"

She nodded.

"Did you kill him?" He asked bluntly.

"No."

"Who did then?" He asked.

"I'm not sure," she lied. "There was a lot going on, lots of shooting. Who are you?"

"I'm Gary's twin. You see, when we were little, we were both sent to foster homes only we didn't get to go to the same one. Gary went to the Simpson's and I went to a different one. He picked the name Braddock out of the air. I chose a different name. I'm not even sure what our real last name was. But when he killed old man Simpson and his wife, Gary found me and we kept in touch through the years."

Jennie felt a cold fear wash over her just hearing him casually say how Gary had callously killed the Simpson's. She struggled at the ropes that had her bound and he laughed. "Gary told me about you. He was head over heels for you and now I can see why."

He sat down by her on the bed and casually caressed her arm, then her face. She tried to turn away and he laughed again. "Don't worry, I'm not Gary. I can keep my hands off of you."

"What do you want Mr..."

"Just call me Jack," he said. "We don't have to be formal here. I was a little surprised when Gary asked us to be the foster parents for your child. At first, I thought maybe it was really Gary's son. But I don't guess that's the case, is it?"

She shrugged her shoulders. "It's possible," she said. "Maybe if he thinks it's Gary's child he won't hurt him," she thought.

He laughed loudly at that. "You're really funny Mrs. Joseph Hall. You see, I know all about you and Joseph. And this is not about any satanic cult. This is strictly about revenge. I'm going to use you and the baby to lure Joseph here so I can get even for Gary's death. And I'll kill three birds with one stone." He left the room laughing at his own wit.

Joseph was getting worried about Jennie. She should have been home by now.

Chavez was getting antsy too. "Hey boss, shouldn't Jennie be here by now?" He asked.

Joseph grabbed his briefcase and opened it up. "Yeah, but I can see where she's at."

"Huh?" Chavez questioned. "What do you mean?"

"I planted a bug in her purse so I could always monitor where she is. I don't want to lose her again." He turned his laptop on to monitor the electronic bug. It was like a tiny GPS system and he could see at a glance which street she was on. "She's still at the diner. Maybe we should go over there and see why she's so late."

When they entered the diner, another waitress was working. "What can I get you fellows?" She asked.

"I'm looking for Jennie, the day waitress." Joseph said.

"There was only one waitress when I got here and her name is Mattie. I don't know who you're talking about."

Joseph grabbed the front of her uniform. "She's my wife and I know she's here. So don't play games with me."

Her eyes widened with fear. "I don't know her, honest."

Joseph flashed his badge, too quickly for her to see that it was a New Orleans badge. "She has a bug in her purse and it's showing that she's here."

"I'll take you in the back and show you that nobody else is here. Even the owner went home for supper."

Joseph saw the lockers in the back and opened each one until he saw her purse on the shelf. His stomach felt like he'd just got on a fast moving elevator going down, and he felt like crying.

He and Chavez paced the floor back at the hotel. They didn't know what to do, where to even start looking for her. "Oh God," he thought, "will all of this cloak and dagger stuff ever end?"

Chapter Twenty-Eight

J ennie lay there with tears running down her face as the horror of the situation sunk in. He would kill them all. He was another Gary, no remorse about killing a human being. She prayed for God to help them, to send His angels to do something, anything. She cast demons out and bound them in Jesus' Name but she didn't think it was helping her situation. "Oh Joseph," she whispered. "How do we always get into these jams? Is our life to be just one big nightmare?"

Jack and the woman were talking in the living room. "What now Jack?" She questioned. "Where do we go from here?"

"I want him to sweat a while when she doesn't come home. I want him to suffer before I contact him and tell him I have his wife and son."

Joseph spoke with Michael Rossi and told him the situation. "Don't worry Joseph," he said. "I'll take care of it. I'll call you when the deed is done."

Nothing to do but wait. Joseph should have been good at that by now but it's not something you get used to when it involves the woman you love with your heart and soul. He thought about the first night he met her. It seemed like she was just a young girl then, she was so sweet and naive. They had come so far together. "Would they have a life together after all?" He wondered.

The phone rang and Joseph went to answer it. It was Michael. "They're on the way up," was all he said.

Joseph opened the door when someone knocked and two Wiseguys entered pushing Carl Jensen in front of them.

"What's the meaning of this?" He cried. "What do you want?"

"I want my wife and son," Joseph answered. "And you're not leaving this room until I find out where they are. If necessary, you won't ever leave the room if you get my drift."

Carl cringed in fear. He knew these were mob people and they didn't threaten casually. "What's it got to do with me?" He asked.

"Don't play games," Joseph said. "People disappear all the time, never to be seen or heard from again. Now, who has my son and is he the same one who has my wife?"

Sweat broke out on Carl's head. "I don't know where he lives. I just call a number and he answers."

"How did you meet him? What's your business with him?" Joseph asked.

"Want me to rub him out boss?" Chavez asked.

Carl was almost crying now. "No, wait. I did an adoption for him, a little boy. He said some people would probably come looking for the kid and I was to let him know when you got here. Said he left a business card somewhere for somebody to find."

"So it was a set up," Joseph thought. "Who would go to the trouble of getting us to come here, and why?" He wondered. Aloud he said, "Give me the number."

Joseph called the phone number and a man answered. His voice sounded vaguely familiar. "This is Joseph Hall. You wanted me to find you. Well I'm here and I want my wife and son."

The man laughed. "Your brassiness doesn't scare me."

"What do you want?" Joseph asked.

"I want you."

Joseph was puzzled. None of this made any sense. "Look," he said, "if it's money you want..."

Jack cut in, "I said it's you I want. I don't want your money, I just want you. And I want you to come alone or your wife and kid will be history. And don't think you can have someone else sneak up on me. I have the area well watched. I'll call you later with the details."

Joseph paced the floor and ran his hands through his hair. He was praying constantly. "Please God, I know that's all you ever hear from me, but Lord, every time I turn around Jennie is disappearing. Is this a normal life for Your servants? Can we ever just have a dull peaceful life?"

Jennie dozed off and on. She saw demons in the room and cast them out. She prayed, she cried, she pleaded with God to save her husband and child. "Oh Lord, we've been through so much, so much evil, so many nightmares. When will it all end? When can we just settle down to a dull life of just casting demons out of your children and setting them free?"

She guessed that as long as the devil was on the earth, God's children would have problems similar to what she and Joseph had to deal with. Of course she couldn't imagine anyone in the world going through what she and Joseph had been through. This had to be unique. Maybe they brought some of it on themselves. However, some of it was just plain evil in the world.

She thought about Joseph's strong arms holding her and she cried. She couldn't bear it if he was killed. She couldn't bear it if Joshua were killed. "Lord, if we have to go, please let me go first so I won't see them murdered before my eyes."

Jennie slept fitfully; dreams of Joseph haunted her. They were dancing and he was kissing her hair, her neck, then his lips found hers. They were riding horses and she longed to have him kiss her. When he finally took her in his arms, his face changed to Gary's face and she woke up drenched in sweat.

Chapter Twenty-Nine

Jack and Gary McRae were, even at four years old, close as twins normally are. They had the same likes and dislikes, the same habits. When their parents were killed and they were separated, they didn't understand not being together anymore.

Gary was placed in a foster home with the Simpson's, and Jack was placed with the Green's. The Green's had three kids of their own and two foster kids in their home already, so little Jack got lost in the shuffle. The other kids bullied Jack and there was no one who showed him the love a little child needed.

By the time Gary found him at sixteen, Jack had all but forgotten him. Then all of a sudden, he had a family, someone of his very own. After Gary left, Jack fantasized about him and Gary making a life together, being a family. That's all he had to hang on to.

Jack always felt a strong love for Gary after the meeting at sixteen. And when Gary found him again at thirty-four, he was willing to do whatever Gary asked of him. Gary was in love with a girl named Jennie, but Joseph always got ahead of Gary in everything he tried to do. Gary's resentment of Joseph became Jack's resentment.

And when Gary called upon him to take the baby, he was glad to be able to do something for his brother. By that time Jack was married so they were prime candidates as foster parents.

They skipped town with the baby and went to Biloxi where they found a lawyer who was willing to overlook the fact that no parent had given up their right to this baby. The lawyer even got someone to sign as the mother, giving permission for them to legally adopt the child.

Jack thought this was one more blow against Joseph, for him to be the baby's daddy. One more strike aimed at Joseph, who Jack resented thoroughly.

Jack was fond of the child but growing up without love, he really didn't know how to love. So his wife provided all the love and care little Joshua needed for his first year in life.

Jack often wondered if Joshua was Gary's baby since Gary hadn't let him be taken by the satanic cult. Jack just figured that he was protecting his own son.

When Gary quit calling, he knew something had happened to him. And Jack took an oath to take revenge on the ones who caused Gary's death. And he knew that it was Jennie and Joseph either directly or indirectly. Now he would get his revenge.

He actually started planning something against them when he left the house they were renting, and hid the business card of the lawyer who was to do the illegal adoption. He hated the two for all they had done to Gary. He knew that somehow, they were even responsible for Gary going to prison for murder. Now, it was his turn to get even.

The phone rang and startled Joseph and the other men in the apartment. Michael Rossi had arranged for some of the Biloxi mob to hang around and help Joseph and Chavez. Carl Jensen, sleeping in the chair he was tied to, came fully awake when it rang. He feared for his life. He had heard enough about the mob to know that they didn't play around with you, just shot you once through the head and dumped the body.

"Hello," Joseph said.

"Go to the Golden Duck bar on the main street along the beach, and be sure you come alone or you'll just find two dead bodies when you get here."

Joseph drove a borrowed car and followed the directions on On Star, the GPS system in the car. He pulled up at the bar, praying all the while. He saw an angel standing near the front door and knew that God was watching over his family and he felt comforted. He also saw demons all over the sidewalk and took authority over them in Jesus' Name.

Once inside, as his eyes adjusted to the darkness of the interior, he stood near the door. He didn't want to rush headlong into anything. He heard a wall phone ringing but didn't really pay it any attention until the bartender asked, "Is your name Joseph?"

"Yeah," he said.

"You have a phone call." The bartender said as he held out the phone to Joseph.

"Come to one twenty three Brighton Place. And be sure and come alone. Or your family will be joining Gary on the other side." He laughed as if he had told a great joke.

Joseph prayed as he had never prayed before. He begged God to help them, to keep Jennie and Joshua safe. "Please God; just give them back to me. Let us continue in our life as it was meant to be, and let us serve You together. Lord, we've been through so much, please have mercy on us."

He drove to the address using the GPS system in the car. He saw more demons here but he also saw angels standing near the front door and felt comforted. He knocked on the door and a woman let him in.

"Is my wife ok?" he asked.

The woman just nodded toward the back of the house and Joseph headed in the direction she nodded. He opened the door and saw Jennie tied up on the bed with a gag in her mouth. Her eyes were big with fear but he didn't take it as a warning, and he felt something hit him on the back of the head. Darkness descended on him and he crumpled to the floor.

When he came to he was tied to a chair in the same room. The door opened and Joseph felt the blood drain from his face when he saw Jack. "Gary?" He questioned, trying to figure out how Gary could still be alive. He shook his head as if trying to clear it.

The man laughed. "That's what she said when she first saw me. Actually, I'm Jack, Gary's twin brother. And you're the man who killed him I assume. My revenge will be complete today. Just killing you is not enough. First, I want you both to suffer. And to that end, I have two guys coming over to pick up your baby. Gary said he was supposed to be sacrificed to the devil but the plans got changed. Well I just re-instated the original plans."

"Noooooo..." Jennie screamed in her mind.

Jack just laughed. He removed the gag out of her mouth then he called to his wife, "Get the door when someone knocks, then bring them in here."

Soon there was a knock on the door and the woman brought the two men to the back bedroom. "Get the baby," Jack told her.

"No Jack, you can't do this. He's my child now. I can't let you do this."

Jack put a gun to her head. "You'll do as I say. Now get the baby."

Jennie looked at Joseph. He was still groggy from the hit on the head. He just sat there with his head hanging and she worried about him.

The woman came back with the baby and handed him to one of the men. They left quickly and Jennie cried, great big sobs of a mother with a broken heart. The woman cried quietly.

Jack pointed the gun at Joseph and fired. Jennie screamed before she blacked out.

Chapter Thirty

Jennie came to and started crying for Joseph, her love, her life. "Oh God," she thought. "How could You let this happen?" She noticed that Joseph was not in the chair any more and she wished that she were dead. She heard men talking in the next room but she didn't care. Let them come and kill her. She had no reason to live now.

She was surprised to see Chavez enter the room and start to untie the ropes that held her. "Chavez, how...?"

"It's ok Jennie. You're safe now."

"But Joseph, oh God, they shot him Chavez." She started crying again as he helped her to sit up in bed.

"Yeah," Chavez said, "they shot him. But he was wearing a bulletproof vest. He's ok Jennie."

"But I don't understand."

Chavez led her into the living room where Jack and his wife were tied up. "Joseph had a bug on himself so we could know where he was at all times. We followed him to the bar, then to this house right away. We weren't sure if Jack would keep him here, or take him someplace else. So we waited until we heard the shot then we busted in."

"But where is Joseph? If he's ok, I want to see him."

"He'll be back. He had some business to take care of." Chavez said.

"Business, what business could be more important than being here with me?"

"Since he was the only one of us who knew what the men looked like who took your son, he wanted to try and catch them before they got too far away."

Joseph took the same car he had used earlier and started driving, praying all the time in his mind. He brought one of the men with him to hold the baby if he was blessed enough to find him.

"Lord, You have to show me where they've taken Joshua. I know it's not Your will for us to lose him again. Send Your angel to show me the way, just like You showed me how to find Jennie when the cult had taken her."

All of a sudden, he heard the word "bus station" in his mind. He used the GPS system to locate the bus station and drove there.

"Wait here." He told the guy with him.

As he walked around looking for them he saw an angel walking near the back of the building and headed in that direction. He saw the two men carrying the baby and he yelled, "Stop those men, they're kidnappers!"

A man standing nearby grabbed the baby from him and another man tripped them when they tried to run. Joseph ran up, badge in hand and showed it to a uniformed cop who was there when the commotion started.

"Officer these men are kidnappers and they were going to use this baby as a sacrifice in their satanic cult. I'm a cop from New Orleans and have been here checking out leads, trying to find this kidnapped baby. There's two more at one twenty three Brighton Place and another at the Lucky Aces, suite 504."

The officer took them into custody and Joseph had his son in his arms for only the second time since he was born.

Jennie started crying again, a reaction from all the stress and strain that she had been under. Chavez just patted her on the shoulder. "There, there Jennie. It'll be ok."

Chavez took her back to the hotel and she was a nervous wreck worrying about Joseph and Joshua. She paced the floor, praying all the time. "Please God, bring them back to me."

Chavez finally convinced her to lie down. She swore she couldn't sleep but the strain had taken its toll on her body and she fell into a deep sleep. She was dreaming that Joseph was kissing her. First one eyelid, then the other. Finally his lips found hers and his kiss transported her to the portals of heaven. She felt him pull her to his chest and murmur sweet love words in her ear. She heard him whisper her name, "Jennie."

It took a while for her mind to grasp it, but she finally realized she wasn't dreaming. Joseph was here, and he was kissing her. And he was whispering her name as he held her.

"Joseph," she said, but he claimed her lips once more and she was lost in his kiss. She was lost in this all-consuming love that she felt for her husband, this love that even the gates of hell could not prevail against. She didn't open her eyes again until she heard the door open, and Chavez entered carrying her son.

Joseph stopped kissing her and took the child from Chavez. He gently laid the baby in Jennie's arms as her tears slid down her cheeks and fell on the child's cheeks. Joseph put his arms around both of them. He finally felt complete, a husband and a father.

And he was ready to serve the Lord. He knew that his faith was strong, and now he could be God's warrior.

He saw the angels standing in the corner and he smiled. God was good to them. They could go forth and serve Him because they had hit bottom—but now they could look up and know that He was always with them. Joseph's faith was complete, and his life was complete.

Everything that he loved in this world was here in his arms.

***"A Light in Darkness" is the prequel to "Embracing the Light" and is due out this year, to be published by Publish America.

<u>Here is an excerpt from A Light in Darkness:</u>

There's a serial killer loose, killing the women from Bourbon street, and Joseph, a vice cop, has to find out who's behind it. Each one is killed the same way—a small knife wound to the heart—almost as if it was made with a dagger. Each of the victims had rope burns on their wrists and ankles. There was no doubt about it; these were ritualistic killings, sacrifices. And now they had Jennie, the woman Joseph loved more than life. And it was up to him to find out where their cult was headquartered, where they held his beloved Jennie, before it was too late.

A Light in Darkness is a mystery novel, but it is also a love story of the passionate love between Jennie and Joseph, a love that even the forces of darkness couldn't stop, as they fulfill the destiny that God has called them to.

A Light in Darkness is the beginning—the beginning of their calling to fight the demonic—the beginning of their love.

***   Watch for the third and final novel in the "Light" series, "Joshua, God's Light in Darkness", a work now in progress.

Printed in the United States
75468LV00006B/44